PROLOGUE

We met six years before in his tattoo shop, KC's INK. I'd come in to get what I call my 'freedom tattoo' between my shoulders. It was a large willow tree with a blackbird flying out of it, meant to symbolize my new beginning—a life free from the shackles of domestic abuse.

He'd smiled at me and winked, making me laugh as he introduced himself. "Hi, I'm Kayleb Cook, but most people call me KC. You can call me anything you want, pretty lady, as long as you call me."

His chiseled Native American features, tattooed body, and long, black hair took my breath away. I knew I was blushing and giggled nervously.

"Smooth, real smooth. I'm Claire Michaels; it's nice to meet you."

We made small talk, comparing musical interests and favorite movies. It turned out we'd both had a soft spot for alternative rock, mainly Red Hot Chili Peppers, Nirvana, and Smashing Pumpkins. I remember how hard he laughed at me when I talked about how much I loved 90s teen movies; he was more of a horror movie fan. I told him about my love of comic books and how I dreamed of opening my own comic book store one day. I ended up telling him about my seven-year-old daughter, and he told me about his fear of fatherhood.

I was curious about his intense expression as he finished my tattoo. He seemed to be deep in thought.

I had to ask. "Are you OK?"

"I'm fine. I'm just trying to figure out why anyone would want to hurt you. Stick with me, beautiful; I'll make sure it never happens again." He put the bandage on my tattoo then ran his finger down my cheek, whispering, "I do believe I'm smitten, Claire Michaels."

Three years later, our love was stronger than I could have ever imagined, and I truly loved my life. I was the bartender at Brown's, the local hot spot, where Kayleb's band *Calvin*—named after his English Bull Dog—played. I'd changed my outfit so many times that night, but I still felt uncomfortable; none of the clothes I'd borrowed felt right. I never had time off for his shows, so I'd wanted to get dressed up for him, but casual was more my style. A true tomboy at heart, I'd take jeans and a band t-shirt over a dress any day. Dressed in my favorite Red Hot Chili Peppers shirt and skinny jeans, I traded in my red high heels for my red Converse. Throwing my long, blonde hair up into a ponytail, I lectured myself while putting on my eyeliner. "Get a grip, Claire; he picked you without all the girlie shit."

"Yes, I did." He'd snuck up behind me and wrapped his arms around my waist. "Stop stressing, pretty lady; I love you just the way you are."

I could still feel his thumb rubbing the tattoo of the Marvel character, Black Widow, on my left forearm, as well as the heat from his soft lips as he covered my freckled nose with tiny kisses.

"I like your shirt, my musical little superhero." Smiling, he'd turned me so we faced the mirror cheek to cheek. "All joking aside, I wish you knew how beautiful you are." Nuzzling my head into his neck, I gave him a sheepish smile. Lovingly, he ran his fingers from the top of my cheek, down the side of my face, and stopped over my heart. "I fell in love with this part of you." Butterflies stirred deep in my stomach as I watched our reflections. Softly kissing my cheek, his hand slid down, massaging my breast. "And it was long before I had the pleasure of knowing this part of you." Gently pinching and pulling my nipple through my shirt, he moved his other hand to the top of my jeans. My heart began to pound as he unbuttoned them, placing just the tips of his fingers underneath. The thought of them moving any farther down made my knees weak. Turning me to face him, his soft tongue gently began to take over my mouth, and his kiss became all I knew. Slowly stepping back toward the bed, he'd whispered, "Let me show you just how irresistible you are."

Later that night, I stood in the audience with my best friend Tyler, watching Kayleb move around the stage, swinging his long hair around as he sang. Although his muscular arms and sculpted abs were enough to make any female melt, it was his deep voice and the slight gap between his teeth that made my heart skip a beat. The set ended and the band thanked the audience before leaving the stage. Kayleb came back on carrying a bar stool and his acoustic guitar, and he sat in the middle of the stage. As the audience clapped and cheered him on, he put his fingers to his lips. "There's a song I want to sing just for my lady!"

As long as you love me, I'll be by your side
I'll be your partner, your lover, your guide
As long as you let me, I'll be right there

Just take my hand baby; we can go anywhere

I'll be your sunshine when your tears fall like rain
Forever your rainbow, I'll heal your pain
As long as you let me, I'll be right there

Just take my hand baby; we can go anywhere
Just take my hand baby; we can go anywhere
Just take my hand baby; we can go anywhere

He put down the guitar and stood up. "Claire, will you come up here with me for a minute?"

I was so nervous by the time I got to the stage that I almost tripped up the steps. Once I was next to him, he leaned in to kiss my flushed cheek. I looked out at the audience, and people were clapping and whistling. Tyler was crying and pointing at Kayleb, who was pulling a small red velvet box out of his pocket, giving me that sweet smile I loved so much. He'd kissed the tip of my nose and got down on one knee. "Claire Madison Michaels, I love everything about you. I knew from the very first day I met you that you were the one for me. Pretty lady, will you marry me?"

I'd held out my shaky hand for him to put the ring on my finger. "Yes! Oh, my god!" I remembered jumping up, wrapping my long legs around him. He stood there holding me, kissing me like nobody was watching. It was our moment—an unforgettable, magical, romantic moment.

He carried me off the stage and walked toward the bar. I nipped at his chin. "Let's go play cowgirl and Indian!"

"Aww, you want more of Daddy's tomahawk?" He'd laughed as he put me down, "I'm going to go say goodbye to the guys first." Pointing at the back room, he smiled. "It looks like someone over there wants to talk to you."

I headed toward the back room and my daughter dove into my arms. "Aunt Tyler let me stay in the back until it was time for Kayleb to ask you." She held her hand up with a big smile. "He asked me if he was allowed to, and when I said yes, he gave me this. He said it's called a promise ring."

I'd held up Audrey's hand. "That's beautiful, sweetheart! We've got ourselves quite the catch, don't we?"

Kayleb scooped my little girl up in his arms. "It's a promise to love and protect you forever. Now I have a princess and a queen!" He kissed Audrey's cheek. "Let's get out of here ladies."

We said our goodbyes and left. On the way home, he held my hand and rubbed his thumb over my engagement ring. "My life is complete now, Claire. I was always happy, but you and Audrey changed everything; you made it brighter. You make life perfect."

I'd closed my eyes to take in the wonder of the night. Was this much happiness even possible? I enjoyed a moment of silence, and then suddenly, my head flew forward. I was horrified when I heard Kayleb scream over the sound of the squealing tires—I can still smell the burnt rubber.

Time seemed to stop and then there was only darkness. I recalled waking up in the ambulance, and I couldn't move my head. There were sounds of muffled voices, but I couldn't make out the words. Fear had overwhelmed me as I tried to catch my breath.

"Where's my daughter? Where's Audrey?" I wasn't sure if the words were coming out or just in my head. "Kayleb, where are you? Where's my fiancé? Where's Kayleb?" Tears fell from my eyes, and my stomach was tied in knots as I tried to understand what was happening. I needed Kayleb, to see him, to touch him, to feel his touch.

The EMT had tried to calm me down but he couldn't; he told me what was happening. "You've been in a car accident. Your daughter is in another ambulance with your friend Tyler. Her father is meeting us at the hospital."

"What about Kayleb? Is he all right?" The silence confirmed the answer I feared. It felt like my heart was being ripped out of my chest.

Kayleb was gone.

CHAPTER 1

Claire

    I sat on the teal suede love seat in the office of Dr. Steven Kelder, tightly gripping my cup of Dunkin Donuts blueberry iced coffee. I rubbed my finger over my right wrist, smiling at the Mighty Mouse tattoo Kayleb had put there for our second anniversary. We wanted to get commitment tattoos, so I got Mighty Mouse because he was Kayleb's favorite character. I love Hulk, so Kayleb got him in the same spot. After the accident, I had wings and a halo put on mine.

    The office was small but cheery. Its bright white walls were decorated with canvas prints full of quotes and lyrics. I'm not sure how many people were encouraged by them; I found them rather annoying. There's only so many times you can read *When Life Gives You Rain, Be The Rainbow* or *When It's Dark, Reach For The Stars* without wanting to throw up. The rug, on the other hand, was one of the coolest things I'd ever seen: it was white with vibrant slices of fruit on it and teal fringes around the edges. The ginger-citrus Yankee Candle he had burning gave the room a spicy yet crisp smell. There was a very modern theme going on. I'd bet his teenage daughter in the pictures on his desk helped pick the decor.

    Gazing out the window at the beautiful blue sky, I wondered why I was still alive. My whole world crumbled that night. Why didn't I die with the two people I loved most? I would have if Kayleb hadn't spun the wheel the way he did. The truck that had dipped into our lane would have hit us head on, but Kayleb made sure it only hit his side. He saved my life. I know now there was more for me to do in life; be it God or Fate, there was a greater plan for me. I wondered if Kayleb was watching me from beyond those soft clouds. Was he watching over Audrey like he promised he would? I wondered if he was disappointed in me for wanting to move on. Did he feel betrayed? I was tired of being alone; I wanted to love and be loved again without guilt. I needed to accept that the feelings I'd developed were okay. Was Audrey upset with me for wanting another child? I'd never stop loving her, but I wanted to be called Mommy again, to feel the bond that only a mother and her child could have.

I almost left this tiny town after the accident so I'd be free of all the reminders of that horrible night. Los Angeles was only a half hour away, and there were so many more opportunities for me. I'd have a fresh start but still be close enough to the people who mattered, but everything was so different. Acceta is a small town, but it's my home. I'm used to the low-key life, not the hustle and bustle of the big city. There was no way I could leave Tyler, either, not after all we've been through in life.

Tyler and I met in the 9th grade, and even though we were complete opposites, we clicked instantly. All through high school she was the beautiful drama club girl all the boys wanted and all the girls wanted to be. I, on the other hand, was a bona fide nerd. I spent all my free time in the photography room or at home reading my comic books. Nowadays, it's cool to be a geek, but back then, getting a boy to look twice at me was impossible. For some reason, Ty was drawn to me—she became my other half—and nobody else mattered to either of us. She was with me through every important stage in my life, the good and the bad. She supported me when I refused to leave my ex-husband Cole, even though she didn't approve of my decision. Once I got the nerve to finally leave him, she was the one who took Audrey and me in. She held my hand when my daughter was born and held *her* as she died. She was one of the first faces my baby saw and the very last one. I know Audrey left this world feeling safe. Tyler is more than my best friend; she's my rock.

So, here I sat on the three-year anniversary of the accident, waiting to pour my heart out to the good doctor. I had been a regular patient for quite a while, but hadn't been here in over a year.

"Ms. Michaels, it's nice to see you." Dr. Kelder entered the room and sat on the matching chair next to me. "How are you today?"

I thought about it as I played with the engagement ring that was still on my finger. I hadn't taken it off since Kayleb put it on. It was simple but so pretty, a rose gold band with chocolate diamonds around it.

"I guess I'm better than I thought I'd be. I just miss them so much." A tear rolled down my cheek as I pictured my little girl; she would have been thirteen this week. "Some people go a lifetime without love, and so many women are unable to have babies. I had both, and for that, I'm thankful." Wiping the tear away, I tried to smile. "I have peace of mind knowing that Kayleb died holding my hand and Audrey was in Tyler's arms, but I wish I could have said goodbye to my little girl. I need to pull myself together though. I've exceeded the acceptable amount of mourning time, and I'm wallowing in self-pity."

"Knowing you're ready is half the battle. The loss of a loved one, especially a child, is not easy to move on from."

"Sometimes I feel guilty for wanting to move on, to be a mom again. I met someone, and he has a five–year-old son I absolutely adore. I feel like I'm betraying Kayleb and Audrey by wanting to be with him. It sounds crazy, but I'm also afraid that if I give myself to another man, something bad will happen. What if I have another child and lose it? It would absolutely kill me to go through all that again."

"Fear is normal, but you can't stop living life. Don't you think

Kayleb would want you to be happy? He died happily in love; don't let yourself die sad and lonely. You're young and beautiful. There is plenty of time left for you to be a mother. So tell me about this person of interest."

"His name is Gavin Price. My friend Tyler tried to hook us up two years ago. They got to know each other because he stops at her coffee shop every morning on the way to work. Through small talk, she found out he was a photography teacher at Acceta Prep School, divorced, and a single father of a three-year-old boy. It had been only a year since the accident, and I had no interest in dating anyone. But since one of my hobbies is photography and that's what he teaches, she decided to play matchmaker. Honestly, the only reason I agreed to go on a date was because he's absolutely gorgeous. We went on a few dates, but when he tried to kiss me, I freaked out, and that was the end of that." I had to smile a little. "Nobody wants to date an emotionally messed up chick who's afraid to be touched by a man. He stayed close though, and now, two years later, except for Tyler, he's my best friend. Tyler calls us the three amigos. I think it's pretty fitting. The way he acts makes me think he wants more, but he might just be a big flirt. Sometimes I wonder if I'll ever get another chance."

"You said he has a son, where is the boy's mother?"

"God knows. She bailed when Miles was two months old. Left a note saying she was going to New York City. She said she never wanted to be a mother, and Miles was Gavin's problem to deal with." I took a sip of my coffee and a deep breath. "Honestly, the bond I've formed with him scares the hell out of me. I love my little monster. If another woman comes into the picture, it will crush me."

"All I can say is be honest. Tell him exactly how you feel. It's really the only way to know where things are. It's a risk you have to take if you want to be with him."

I knew he was right, but it was easier said than done. What if I'd missed my chance? I could lose my best friend.

"How is work going? Are you still working for the lawyer you were unhappy with?"

I had quit the bar after the accident and got a job as an assistant at Genniti, Genniti & Marks. They were the only good lawyers in Acceta, and the Genniti brothers knew it. Jana Marks was their older sister, a married mother of four who was a pit bull in the courtroom and a total sweetheart once she left it. Joseph Genniti was a middle-aged, overweight, alcoholic. He had two kids, three ex-wives, and a serious hatred of women. Three divorces later, you'd think he'd pick up on the fact that *he* might be the problem. I worked for their younger brother, Anthony Genniti. As good looking as he was, he's an alpha male douchebag who thought just because he gave me my paycheck, he could put his hands on me. I could tell he was one of those guys who pictured a woman naked as she walked by them. Toward the end, I'd started carrying mace in my purse. I was so happy to be out of there.

"When I got the settlement from the accident, I bought KC's INK and re-opened it. I don't do tattoos, but I rent out two chairs. I recently added an expansion and turned it into a comic book store. I always wanted to do that, but my ex-husband told me I was stupid for it, that comics were for children and men. I have to say it's great being my own boss."

"Well, I'm glad you are following your dreams. I think it's time for a change in your personal life now. You know you're ready. Pick a good place to start. Take baby steps if it makes you more comfortable. Why don't you think about moving your ring? If you don't want to take it off completely, maybe put it on the other hand or on a necklace. Think of it as a new beginning while still embracing the past you love."

I had plans to meet Tyler and Gavin for dinner, so I said my goodbyes to Dr. Kelder and headed home to get changed. We passed on our usual Ace's Diner to try La Pinnoti, the new Italian restaurant. It's one of the few fancy places in town, so I figured I'd dress up a bit. I dug through my closet and settled on a tight little sleeveless red dress Tyler had left at my house. My black boots made me look somewhere between sexy and a hooker, but I knew Gavin would love it. I threw on some eyeliner and red lipstick, and I was out the door.

They already had a table when I got there, and I headed toward them. They looked like the perfect couple, both utterly gorgeous. Tyler has long, wavy, raven black hair that falls to the middle of her back. Her fair skin makes her big, emerald-green eyes stand out. She has full lips, perfect for the red lipstick she always wears, and men are always looking at her curvy body. She's never liked the attention; she hasn't had a boyfriend in years. She prefers the scruffy biker type and there aren't a lot of men like that in Acceta. She always says she's saving herself for Jared Leto...as long as he keeps his beard.

Gavin has a bit of a bad boy look to him and is the proud owner of a black and silver Harley Davidson Road King. He has soft, honey-blond hair, about chin length; I love running my fingers through it and tucking it behind his ears. His beard is just long enough to pull on but not what you'd call a full beard, and I melt when he smiles so big that his dimples show. His eyes are enchanting, a crystal blue with specks of green and beautiful blond eyelashes that most women would kill for. Its crazy how just pulling his hair back and putting on a dress shirt can instantly turn him from a biker to a prep school teacher. I can't believe this incredibly sexy man wanted me, and I blew it by pushing him away. Now I'm in the friend zone. At least it's a flirty friend thing; it makes most people assume we're a couple.

"Hey there beautiful! Nice legs, I mean nice dress." He gave me a wink and pulled out my chair, kissing my cheek as I sat. "I have good news, baby girl. I got you a meeting with the gallery owner I was telling you about. They're having an expo the night before Halloween, and if she likes your stuff, you're in. She gave me her number to give to you, and I hope you don't mind but I gave her yours."

Tyler laughed. "Come on Gav, we all know the number was for you."

"Thanks Gav, I don't even know what to say. Although I must say I'm impressed by your ability to dazzle women into doing things for you." I gave him an evil smile and blew him a kiss. "So tell me, did you use those eyes of yours, your adorable dimples, or did you introduce her to your little friend?"

"No worries, love. All nine inches of my not-so-little friend are waiting patiently to dazzle you!"

Tyler shook her head. "You two should just do it already because you make me want to puke."

"So I saw my shrink today. Let's just say I'm done stressing over things. The past is the past, and I can't keep delaying my future on account of it. You can't betray the dead, and I'm not trying to die alone and full of regret because I'm too afraid to change my ways."

Tyler reached over and hugged me. "I'm so proud of you, Claire. I know it hasn't been easy, but it's time. We need to get our shit together before we're officially considered cougars."

"Umm, does the single dad get in on this club? Even better, I could break it up." He gave me his mischievous smile and raised an eyebrow. "I do have to bail on you ladies, I've got parent/teacher conferences this evening."

Tyler stuck her tongue out. "You just don't want to pay for dinner, you cheap ass!"

"Here woman." Gavin threw his credit card at her as he stood up. "I'll get it back tomorrow, and no shopping after dinner, either." He wrapped his fist inside my long, blonde hair and gently pulled my head back. "If you want to buy something I can rip off with my teeth then feel free."

"Maybe I will. I know you like me in red. So tell me, hot stuff, do you prefer satin or lace?"

Releasing my hair, he whispered in my ear, "I hope you know you're driving my not-so-little friend crazy right now."

"Well, aren't you a class act, Mr. Price?" I smiled, trying to ignore the butterflies fluttering in my stomach.

Tyler stuck her finger down her throat. "Enough already."

He kissed my forehead and gave Tyler a hug before he left. We had another glass of wine and went our separate ways.

Somehow, on the way home, I ended up at Brown's. I hadn't stepped foot in there since the night of the accident; it was too painful. Dr. Kelder had a good point about moving on with everything, and this was the first step. I took a deep breath and walked in the door, scanning the room for a familiar face. I saw my old boss, Dave, by the pool table trying to pick up a young twenty-something. He looked the same as he did the last time I saw him, like George Clooney in *From Dusk till Dawn* but with an Irish accent. He had all the girls with daddy issues eating out of his hand. He ran toward me and scooped me up.

"Blondie, how ya' been, doll?"

"Damn Dave, I have a dress on; you're showing the

customers my lady parts."

"What have we here? My blondie is all dressed up!"

"Well, don't get used to it." I looked toward the girl. "I see some things never change. At least that one looks old enough to be in the bar."

"Barely. If she's telling the truth, she's twenty-one. With tits like that, who cares?"

"Am I cock-blocking? I'll let you get back to Big Boobs McGee."

"No way, blondie. Girls like her are a dime a dozen. You've got my full attention. Where's your partner in crime? I figured the two of you finally came out of the closet, got hitched, and were off starting a family."

There wasn't any hiding what Ty and I did; plenty of people knew about our fling. If I could go without dick in my life, Tyler would be my wife by now.

I told him all about my visit with Dr. Kelder and how I need a fresh start. "I'll always love Kayleb; he helped me out of my shell. He taught me to be myself no matter what anyone had to say, and he loved me for me. It's time for me to realize its okay to move on. I want to feel the touch of a man who wants me and not feel like I'm doing something wrong." I saw the empty stage and went and sat on it. I twisted my ring back and forth as the memory of that night ran through my head. The way he sang to me, the way he looked when he was down on one knee, how my hands shook as he put the ring on my finger, and the kiss that I didn't know would be our last.

"The last time I was up here, I was getting this put on my finger."

Dave went to the jukebox and chose the song Kayleb had sung to me. Tears welled up in my eyes when I heard his voice, and everyone around me seemed to fade from existence. I saw Kayleb sitting on the stage, singing like he had that night. It felt so surreal, warm, and painful at the same time. He looked like an angel, so full of light. I tried to touch him, but I was frozen. The song ended, and he knelt beside me. "It's time to let me go, sweetheart. I'll see you again one day, but you need to live your life. I'll always be with you, but you need to give your heart to someone else, be the mother you deserve to be again. Audrey and I will be waiting for you, together." I felt a warm sensation on my cheek and then, just like that, he was gone. A strange sense of peace flowed through me as I kissed my ring and moved it to the other hand.

"I'm proud of you, doll. I know this isn't easy for you. He was a good man, and he loved you both very much. Your baby is in good hands, and this is the closure you need. I'm glad my blondie is back."

****

I got home and kicked off my boots. My whole body ached, so I went upstairs and drew myself a hot bath. I put on some music and surrounded myself in the soft scent of lavender bubble bath.

Nothing soothes me more than alternative music from the 90s. I can't explain it, but it takes me to another place. The guitar is like a safe haven for me. Kayleb taught me how to play it, enabling me to become a part of the magic that moved me. I haven't picked my guitar up since he died. It's just hanging on my living room wall. I dipped my head under the water and let it all go.

I climbed into bed with Calvin and turned on the TV. He nuzzled his fuzzy face in my neck and covered me with slobbery kisses. As we snuggled up, I flipped the channels until I found a marathon of *Hard Law*. I loved Winston Ryan, the actor who played Agent Vince Elliot. He was an undercover cop in a badass motorcycle club who worked his way up to VP. Kayleb bought me a red *Mrs. Vince Elliot* shirt as a joke, but it's actually one of my favorites. I turned out the lights and, after such a long day, fell right to sleep.

CHAPTER 2

Claire

I woke up ready to start my new life, the new version of the old me. I called Tyler and asked her meet me at our usual Dunkin Donuts for coffee so I could tell her about my emotional breakthrough. Ready for my lazy day, I threw on yoga pants and a tank top, wrapped my hair in a messy bun, and headed out the door. I got there first, so I grabbed our usual fix, blueberry iced coffee. Just as I sat down, she got there and joined me.

"Thank you, love. Boy, we are creatures of habit."

I told her all about what happened at Brown's and the vision of Kayleb. "I know it sounds crazy Ty, but it all seemed so real. I felt such a sense of peace afterward, like a huge weight had been lifted off my shoulders, and I got the closure I've needed. I'll never be able start a new chapter in life if I keep re-reading the last one." I showed her that I'd moved my ring off my left ring finger and lifted my coffee in the air. "So, here's to a new beginning. Now I have to figure out how to tell Gavin how I feel. This flirty friendship we have is all in good fun, but I want more. If I 'fess up to it and he doesn't feel the same way, I risk losing him, and if I lose him, then I lose Miles. If he wanted more, he would have tried by now."

"You need to cut all the sexual tension and give the man some of that sweet ass. The poor guy's eyes bulge every time he sees it."

"Well, a lady never makes the first move."

"Being a lady is overrated; get yourself a big ol' penis. Besides, he made the first move years ago. How about an old school girl's night? You, me, Freddy Prinze Jr., and some Honey Jack!"

"Sounds great. *She's All That* and intoxication begin at 6 o'clock."

"I need to get to the shop now. One of my girls called out again, so I'm there until five. This chick is pissing me off with all her excuses. If she wasn't a single mom, I'd have canned her ass months ago."

"You're too damn nice. Random thought: you own your own coffee shop so why do we always meet here?"

"Because I end up working any time I enter my lovely Java Spot. Later, love!"

I was bored and had the itch to do something fun, so I called Gavin to see if I could steal Miles for the day. I loved taking Miles out; it made me feel like a mom again. I loved the way he looked at me with those innocent little eyes. We both filled the hole in each other's hearts. It was such a great feeling when someone came up and told me how cute my son was. All I ever did was say thank you. As childish as it seems, I loved pretending he was mine.

I pulled up to the house, and he came running out and jumped into my arms. "Hey, love bug, are you ready for some fun?"

He squeezed me tight and kissed my cheek. "I missed you, Mommy!"

I looked at him, and his eyes immediately hit the ground. This poor kid just wanted a mom to love him. I didn't get how she could just walk away and not look back, although I'm glad she did because now I have him.

"Miles, we can talk to Daddy about whether or not you can call me that. I don't mind, but he has to say it's okay first." I gave him a big hug and kiss. "I love you so much, sweetie, and I promise I'll never leave you, no matter what you call me. You'll always be my little love bug, even when you're all grown up."

Gavin came outside. "Any way I can get you to let me play third wheel? I know my boy is your date, but I'd like to tag along. Maybe he can show me how to get the girl."

Miles laughed and grabbed both of our hands. "You can come, Daddy, but she's mine."

He tussled the boy's hair and smiled at me. "I guess Mr. Miles gets the final decision!"

"Daddy, can Claire be my mommy? I know she's not my real mommy, but I wish she was."

Awkward doesn't begin to explain how I felt. "Gav, I'm not sure what I'm supposed to say here. I don't mind; honestly, I'd love it. Realistically speaking though, once you find the right girl, she's going to want that title. I understand if it's reserved for the future Mrs. Gavin Price."

He bent down to his son's level and looked him in the eyes. "If you want Claire, buddy, you've got her." Standing up, he hugged me and whispered in my ear, "Thank you for loving him."

"I'm dressed like a total bum, so we can't go just anywhere. I'm thinking Bounce World. How's that sound, love bug?" He loves that place. I'm not gonna lie, so do I. I used to take Audrey there all the time. The place is all bounce houses and trampolines big enough for adults to enjoy, also.

"Miles, I think your mommy looks very pretty, even when she's dressed like a bum." Giving me a wink, he smiled. "Let's bounce! I'm driving though; my truck misses you.

The last time I was in his truck, I was drunk out of my mind. I guess I'd had a few too many shots of Fireball. Gavin says I was making out with the dashboard and telling the truck how sexy it was. Honestly, I don't remember that part. I do love it though. It's a black Ford F150 Raptor, and it really is just as sexy as its owner.

****

The three of us jumped around that place for what seemed like hours until the basketball section finally did me in. I jumped off the ledge and tried to dunk it but fell flat on my face instead.

They simultaneously yelled, "Mommy down!"

"Thanks boys. Can I get a hand?"

Gavin reached out to help me up, but Miles pushed him down right on top of me. He pushed his upper body up and stared at me for a minute, giving me his beautiful smile that made his dimples show. "If we weren't in public, I might take full advantage of this position." He rubbed his nose against mine. "I could do some very naughty things to you right now." He kissed my forehead and did a push-up to roll off me. He helped me up and smacked my ass as we climbed out of the bounce house, making me yell unintentionally. "We should go. Mr. Monster looks like he needs a nap."

The man was one of my best friends, my shoulder to cry on. If I try for more, and he doesn't feel the same way, then I could lose him. I had my chance, and I pushed him away. I blew it. There was only one way to find out if he wanted more than this playful friendship. I had to suck it up and ask. Miles fell asleep so I figured it was time. I mustered up the courage, but just as I opened my mouth to speak, he interrupted me.

"Why are you so good to him? You treat him like he's yours

even though we're only friends. I'm grateful for it, but sometimes I wonder why you do all you do for us."

"Gav, no child should be without a mother. He's so sweet and easy to love; it just feels so right. You just need to tell the next chick she's back burner in my boy's eyes. You're stuck with me for the long haul, Mr. Price. I'm the baby mama!"

"God help me!" He started laughing then grabbed my hand to kiss it.

Once we got back to the house, he gave me a tight hug before I got into my car. I wanted to stay right there in his arms, for him to hold me like that and never let go. With a kiss to my forehead, he opened my car door for me.

"Why do you always kiss my forehead? I don't mind, but I never see you do it to Ty, and you do it to me all the time."

"Honestly, Grammy always says a kiss on the forehead is much sweeter than a thousand kisses on the lips. They are full of love and respect instead of pure lust."

I gave him a slightly embarrassed smile then got into my car. Driving home, my face was probably as red as my little red Cabrio. I tried not to make too much of it since he'd said it so casually, but I instantly had butterflies in my stomach hearing those words.

Tyler showed up about an hour late; she's the type that will be late for her own funeral.

"I know I'm late; stop giving me the stink eye. I brought Honey Jack and Captain, girlie. What's your poison?"

"I'll go with the Cap tonight." I spaced out for a few minutes. I couldn't stop thinking of Gavin. My body started to tingle as I thought about his body on top of me, about his strong arms on each side of my face. The words he said kept running through my mind, and I could still feel him holding me close.

Tyler grabbed the cups and started making our drinks. "Okay, spill it woman."

"What are you talking about?"

"Claire, I've been your friend for over two decades. I can read you like a book. Do you really think I can't tell that something is going on in that pretty little head of yours? I have a real good idea of what it is, but I want to hear you say it."

"You're crazy, Ty!"

She started blowing little kisses at me. "Whatever you say, Mrs. Price."

"Oh my God, are you twelve?"

"Well, I'm tired of seeing my two best friends fight the inevitable. It's obvious that you both want the same thing. All the cute flirting has turned into straight sexual tension lately. You need to stop being so scared of rejection. The man has turned down over a dozen women just waiting on you. He's the sweetest guy I know, and he's sexy as hell, so what's the hold up?"

"I don't want to lose him, Ty. Say I did get him, it would kill me if it didn't work out. It's safer to just stay friends."

"That's bullshit and you know it. You've been crazy about him for such a long time, and now that you're ready to accept it, you come up with this friend zone crap. What happens when he's tired of waiting? Are you going to be able to handle watching the man you love be with another woman? Do you want someone else playing mommy to Miles, or are you gonna woman up and take what's yours?"

"Jesus, you're brutal. I spent all day with them today. We went to Bounce World. Miles called me mommy, and it just felt so right. I was going to pour my heart out on the way home, but before I could, Gavin asked me why I was so good to Miles since we're only friends. He doesn't feel the same way, Ty. He's just a flirt. I guess I waited too long for my second chance."

"Fuck the movie, let's get drunk."

Half way through our bottle of Captain, we found ourselves singing and dancing to Ol' Dirty Bastard and reminiscing about Ty's old flames, I didn't have any to talk about, so we stuck to hers. It felt so good to escape reality for a little bit until the doorbell rang.

Tyler peeked out the window. "It's Gavin."

"Did you invite him, Ty? Don't lie to me."

She shook her head no and opened the door. He looked a bit disappointed to see her and surprised to see me drunk.

"Hey, Ty, I hope I'm not interrupting an estrogenfest."

She pulled him in by his shirt. "It's cool homie, since you're one of the girls."

I get serious word vomit when I'm drunk, so I tried to sober up real quick, but it wasn't happening. "What are you doing here? I mean, I wanted you here, but I wasn't expecting it to actually happen. Goddamn, you look sexy! Oh shit, did I just say that out loud?" I could feel my face turning red from embarrassment.

"Why yes, you did say that out loud. I wanted to talk to you about something, but we can wait until you sober up. I know how your filter disappears when you drink, so let's watch a movie or something before you spill all your secret thoughts about me."

I hopped onto his lap and cuddled into his strong, muscular chest. I could feel his lips graze my hair as he breathed in the scent of my vanilla shampoo. Smiling at him gave me butterflies in my stomach, and being in his lap sent a rush of desire I was trying so hard to hide.

He put his lips to my ear and whispered, "You smell so good, baby girl, like warm sugar."

Tyler put on *She's All That* and turned out the lights. "It's time for us to school you in the art of high quality cinema."

The liquor had given me the guts to climb onto his lap, but halfway through the movie, I sobered up enough for it to be awkward. He didn't seem to mind though. As a matter of fact, he seemed perfectly fine with it. Why does this man make me feel so giddy? I ran my fingers through his hair and tucked it behind his ear.

He whispered into my ear, and his voice stirred a warm sensation deep inside. "I'm here because I just needed to see you. I dropped Miles off at my mom's and took a chance you'd be home. We have a lot to talk about, love, but I need you totally sober first." He nibbled on my earlobe and ran his thumb across my bottom lip. "I had an awesome time today. I'm not sure who had the bigger smile on his face, my son or me. Either way, it was you who put it there, I just wanted to say thank you for all you do for us." He kissed my forehead, and I nuzzled into his neck to watch the movie.

The end credits started to roll, and Tyler turned on the lights. "Well, what did you think?"

"I guess it wasn't bad for a chick flick, but it's far from high quality cinema."

I started to scoot off of him, and he pulled me back onto his lap. "Where do you think you're going? I'm not ready to let you go yet!"

"On that note, I'm going to bed. Have fun you two. I'm crashing in the spare room."

Before I knew it, he was flipping me over onto the couch and climbing on top of me. My entire body went limp as he kissed me; his lips were so soft. His tongue swept over mine, and I ground my hips against him. Wrapping his fist in my hair, he pulled my head back, biting and kissing down my neck. I couldn't hold back my whimpers and moans as I felt his erection pressing against my body.

"I need you inside me, please."

He took me upstairs to my room and threw me onto the bed, pulling my pants down so quickly that my panties came down with them. Standing at the foot of the bed, he ran his fingers up and down my inner thigh.

"I've waited a long time to touch you, Claire, to feel your soft pussy around me. I'm not going to fuck you right now, even though I want to more than anything. I need you to be sober."

"Then why would you bring me up here? Why did you start this?"

Looking into my eyes, he shoved two fingers deep inside me, circling and stretching me. Smiling at me, he pulled out his fingers, licking my arousal off them. He gave me a smug, cocky look and pulled me to the edge of the bed.

"Because I'm hungry."

My eyes flew open as I sat up quickly with a smile on my flushed face. I noticed the movie was just about over when Tyler beaned me in the head with a pillow.

"This bitch can't drink anymore if she can't even stay awake through her favorite movie. Dude, you suck!"

Gavin squeezed my leg playfully. "Judging by the rosy cheeks and the smile while you were sleeping, I'd say someone was having a really nice dream! I hope it was about me since you were all cuddled up on my lap."

"You wish, ya jerk."

"Yes I do! So tell me, darlin', did I perform well? I'd hate to leave you unsatisfied."

"I'm sure I'll be just fine. It's late; do you want to stay?"

"I don't know if that's a good idea."

"Please Gav, I'd really like to fall asleep next to you tonight."

Smiling at me, he grabbed my hand and walked me up to my room. Stripping to his boxers, he climbed into my bed and slipped under the blanket. I slowly undressed in front of him, leaving on only my white lace boy-short panties. He only smiled a little bit, so I put on a tank top and climbed into bed next to him. Pulling me to his chest, he whispered, "Good night, baby girl." His long fingers ran through my hair as he kissed my forehead, keeping his lips against me until I fell asleep.

My dream came in flashes, like a slideshow in my head. I saw it play out from beginning to end, the good, the bad, and the ugly. It was like a beautiful dream being consumed by a horrible nightmare.

I saw the first time I met Cole. We were in our freshman year of college and he was just as out of place at that party as I was. I was the shy, nerdy type, and he was the serious, sophisticated one. He was so handsome. I couldn't stop staring at him.

I saw our first date. He was so sweet and charming. He had asked me out for dinner and a movie, and he showed up at my door with a picnic basket full of Chinese takeout and his laptop computer. He kissed me that night—my very first kiss—under a willow tree as we watched *The Breakfast Club*.

I saw us lying under the stars under the same tree on graduation night. That was the night Cole proposed to me. The smile on my face didn't go away for weeks.

I saw my wedding day. I watched myself walk toward my first love, ready to give him my life. His gorgeous face was full of excitement and wonder. His warm eyes and soft smile were so enchanting, and our wedding night would be in my mind forever.

I saw Audrey's birth, the greatest day of my life. Cole was so afraid that I had to promise him she wouldn't break before he'd hold her. Then I watched the strongest man I knew turn into a puddle of mush in a second.

The flashes got darker, more intense, and terrifying.

I saw our first fight. Audrey was two. I told him I wanted to go back to work, and he told me it was out of the question. I argued my point, but that got me a busted lip, and he squeezed my neck so hard I had to wear a scarf for a week.

I saw myself walking around with my sunglasses permanently attached to my face; I was always thankful for the California sun. The physical pain hurt but was easier to bear; the bruises always healed. It was the emotional pain that almost killed me. I lost myself and became an insecure mess.

I saw myself curled up in the corner crying as he fucked other women in front of me. He'd always said it wasn't cheating if I was in there to watch it happen.

I saw him leave us to go to her and come back covered in scratches and smelling like her perfume. There were many women, but she was the constant—the beautiful Lark. I always felt like nothing when she looked at me, like a piece of trash tossed to the ground.

I saw the final blow. He was on top of me, tearing my clothes off. The more I tried to fight him off the harder he hit me. All I could smell was whiskey and my own blood. Grabbing my face, he yelled, "You can't rape your own wife; shut up and take it." I wanted it to be over, so I lay there and let him finish.

I saw myself grab my daughter and run... I never looked back.

I woke up screaming. "No, stop! Get off me, Cole! I hate you!"

Gavin shot out of bed, blood gushing from his nose. He grabbed me and held me close, pulling me into his arms.

"Tyler, get in here! Help me!"

"Jesus Christ, Gavin, what happened?"

"She had a nightmare." He sat there kissing the top of my head, rocking me back and forth as he kissed my forehead. "Tell me it was just a dream, Claire, all you said in your sleep. Please baby, tell me he didn't rape you." His eyes burned with anger and his fists clenched. "I'll kill him with my bare hands, I swear I will."

"It happened a long time ago; it's what made me finally leave him. You need to let it go. He's an LAPD Detective. If you do anything to him, you'll end up in jail."

Tyler was standing there crying. "Why didn't you tell me? I would have helped you."

"You would have made me go to the cops; they'd never believe me over him. I was ashamed that I didn't leave him the first time he put his hands on me. I was angry with myself for becoming so weak. Now all my dirty laundry is out. I'm a mess."

The three of us cuddled in my bed, and they held me until we all fell asleep.

I woke up the next morning to my phone buzzing. I broke from their embrace but woke them in the process. "It's a text from your gallery lady. She wants to meet me Saturday morning."

"Awesome! Do you want me to come with you?"

"No, but I'll have you meet me after. This is amazing; I owe you big time. Thank you guys for last night. I love you both so much."

"I have to go get Miles, but I'm going to call and check on you later." He gave me a peck on the forehead and whispered, "Sweeter than a thousand!"

Tyler headed toward the stairs. "I need coffee."

"I'm sorry I didn't tell you."

"I probably would have gone to jail for cutting his balls off. How do you even look at him? Jesus, Claire, you're Supergirl."

"Hell, no!" I held out my arm and pointed to my tattoo. "I'm Black Widow, bitch!"

We laughed as we grabbed our coffee and headed to the living room. Tyler curled up next to me on the couch and turned on the TV. "Nothing like some Maury in the morning to make your life seem normal!"

"Before you ask, nothing happened last night before my nightmare. I practically begged him to stay. He can't resist my pouty face. I just had to be next to him after... the dream I had on his lap."

"Shut up!"

"Yeah, I was hoping he'd try something, but he didn't. I even got undressed in front of him, right down to the panties. He wasn't taking the bait, so I put a shirt on and we cuddled. At least I got to feel his skin on mine."

"Holy shit, I can't believe he called it. As far as him not taking the bait goes, you were drunk; he didn't want to take advantage of you. I know for a fact he wants you. He's borderline obsessed with you. So tell me, was the dream sex good?"

"I didn't get any. We were kissing and touching, and then he said he was hungry. I woke up just as he was about to go down on me.

"Oh, my God!" She was laughing uncontrollably. "I'll never be able to keep a straight face the next time he says the word 'hungry'."

CHAPTER 3

Claire

    I woke up Wednesday not sure of how my day would go. It was the day my daughter would have turned thirteen. I thought about staying in bed all day, which would just depress me more. I tried to watch TV, but nothing held my interest enough to stop the pain. After forcing down a cup of coffee, I decided to go for a run to clear my head. I scooped up the dog leash to take Calvin along with me even though it would be more of a fast paced walk with him. We headed for the dog park a few blocks away. He always had a blast there. My phone rang, but I ignored it, I wasn't in the mood to talk to anyone. I thought about my thirteenth birthday party. My mom tried to make it so special, but only two people came. I wondered what Audrey would have been like. I pictured her as a young Avril Lavigne, a musical little alternative type. She looked so much like me at ten; what would she look like now? Would Kayleb and I have had a child? These were all questions that would never be answered.

    As soon as we got there, Calvin made friends with a little yorkie that was just as annoying as his owner. The girl irked me; she was a total plastic.

    "Hi, I'm Sasha, and this is Petey" She actually lifted the dog and had him wave his paw at me.

    "I'm Claire, and this is Calvin."

    She started with small talk about nothing important, and I tuned out most of what she was saying. I instantly regretted wearing a tank top because she kept touching my tattoos, asking what they meant and if they hurt. I found myself wishing my dog would eat her. My phone rang and I was thankful to have a polite reason to step away. I was hoping it was Gavin, but it was Cole.

"Hello, Cole."

"I just wanted to call and see if you were all right today."

"I'm doing okay; I've got a lot on my plate lately, so it's keeping me busy. How are you doing?"

"I'm okay, I guess. I just miss her so much. I wanted our life together to be different. My mind has been stuck on 'what if' today."

"Well, you can't change the past, but you can make a future you'll be happy in. Thanks for calling to check on me, and for giving me the prettiest, little girl in the world.

"You're welcome! Of course, she was beautiful; she looked just like you."

"Have a good day Cole, and thanks again."

"Bye, Claire"

I hung up the phone and wiped my watery eyes. So many bad things happened with Cole, but there were so many good memories, too, before the alcohol consumed him and stole the Cole I'd given my life to. Hearing him sound so sad broke my heart. Even though he'd put me through hell, part of me would always feel for him. He was the first man I gave all of myself to. He was my first love, my first kiss. Not only did I give him my virginity, I also gave him his only child. I really wish I could still hate him, but it's not in my nature. I know he's hurting right now just as much as I am; she was his daughter, too.

"Are you all right?" Sasha tilted her head and gave a fake smile.

Like I'm going to tell this chick any of my business. "I'm fine. It's just one of those days."

I looked at the screen saver on my phone. It was a picture of Gavin, Miles, and me taken Christmas morning last year. I wondered if I'd ever be Gavin's missing piece, not just a fill-in until he finds someone else.

"Is that your son? He's adorable!"

"Kind of, I'm the only mom he has; his name is Miles."

"My son's name is Adam. I knew you looked familiar; our boys are in the same class. His daddy sure is easy on the eyes!"

"Yeah, he's kind of cute."

"Girl, your dog is cute; your man is sexy."

"Thanks. I got to get going. I'll see you around."

I think I just told that girl that Gavin and I were together. Whatever. Maybe she'll stay away from him. As annoying as she was, she's too pretty to compete with.

I decided to walk a mile to the cemetery to visit Audrey's grave. When I arrived, Cole was there. I walked up next to him, and he hugged me tightly. That was the first time I let him touch me since I left him other than at Audrey's funeral. He sank to the ground, sobbing. This put-together man was crumbling in my arms. We just sat on the ground together as I held him, rubbing his hair.

"Claire, I'm a wreck. I haven't been able to sleep lately, and when I do, I keep dreaming of the night you left. I'm so sorry. I should be in prison for what I did to you. How can you even look at me?" He sat up and wiped his eyes. "I need you to know I'm not that guy anymore. I haven't touched a drink since the night Audrey died. I'm the man you fell in love with, not the monster you left. I know I ruined everything; I'll never find anyone like you. I don't want to, either. I want you. Please give me another chance, love. I'm begging you. I can make us what we should have been."

I ran my hand down the side of his face and kissed his cheek. "I'll always love you, Cole. You've gotten every first a girl has to give. You made me a mother, the greatest gift anyone could give. You have to know I can never be with you again; too much has happened between us." I held his hand in mine. "I forgive you, and I'm proud of you for conquering your demons, but there has been too much lost for us to ever make it work. Why don't we get up, and you can take me out for lunch. We can talk about our little girl."

"I'm good with lunch for now, but I'll never get over you. I was a twisted asshole, and I lost the two greatest gifts I was ever given because of it. I know you found a man you feel is better, and I respect that, but deep down, I'll always believe in us. I'll wait for you forever.

We went to Gala's Cafe for lunch since they had outdoor dining and I had Calvin with me. We ate our lunch and laughed about the good times we once had. I had to admit it was good to see the change in him, to see the old Cole again. A part of me wondered what I would have done if I wasn't in love with Gavin.

He grabbed my hand and kissed it. "Maybe we can do this again next year, unless you decide we can do it sooner. You know my number." He kissed my cheek, and we parted ways.

I went home to shower and get to the shop so I could actually get some work done on my portfolio. I was still so excited that Gavin had set this up for me. My pictures might actually be part of this huge expo. Once I was in the shower, I thought about Gavin and

Miles, about how it felt every time I was with them. I decided I was going to ask them to spend the night, and then I'd ask Gavin for forever.

CHAPTER 4

Gavin

I pulled into the parking lot of Acceta Elementary School, still baffled over what I'd seen on the way here. Cole and Claire together, smiling, hand-in-hand, his lips on her cheek. What world am I in right now? Stressing doesn't even cover what I'm feeling: I'm furious. I guess I was wrong about her wanting me. How could she do this? We aren't together, but to pick him over me is an insult.

I got out of the car to get Miles, and one of the moms came toward me. I'd seen her here, but we'd never spoken. She is very pretty but young. Her curly, red hair flowed to the bottom of her butt and her white sundress hung only a few inches below it. Unlike Claire, this girl didn't leave much to the imagination. The doors opened, Miles came running out, and a little boy skipped over to her as she smiled at me.

"Hi, my name is Sasha. My son, Adam, is always talking about playing with Miles. I was wondering if we could set up a play date this weekend. I should probably talk to your wife; I wouldn't want her to get mad or anything.

"Well, my ex-wife is somewhere in New York City and has probably forgotten she had a son. The girl who brings Miles in the morning is my best friend Claire. I'm the one to talk to about getting together."

As soon as the words came out of my mouth, everything about her changed. She pushed her breasts out and sucked in her non-existent belly. Walking back to the parking lot, I couldn't help but notice her tight little ass swaying side to side, for my benefit no doubt. I was flattered by her need for my attention. The boys said goodbye, and Miles hopped in the truck. When I reached to buckle him in, she pulled my phone out of my back pocket.

"Hey now, darlin', personal space."

"Sorry, I was just putting my number in it so we can get the boys together this weekend. If you'd like, we can set up a play date of our own; I'm free tonight."

"Maybe we can arrange that. By the way, my name is Gavin. I'll call you later and let you know."

I got into the truck and started the engine. As amused as I was over what had just happened, I couldn't shake my anger with Claire. I'd waited all this time for something that apparently would never happen. It was time to drop the idea of Mrs. Gavin Price. Now the trick would be keeping our friendship together. I needed to talk to Tyler; she'd know what to do. I headed toward the Java Spot, hoping Claire wouldn't be there. With KC's right next door, she was there all the time. I was in the clear; her little red Cabrio was nowhere to be seen.

"Hey boys! The usual for my homie and a chocolate cupcake for the kiddo. What's wrong Gav? You've got serious anger face on right now. Who pissed in your lemonade?"

Ty had a way with words; she could always make me smile.

"There's that pretty boy smile I love to see!"

"Yeah, pretty boy my ass."

She handed me a large black coffee and a cupcake for Miles. She set him up at the table next to us with her IPod and some coloring things. "Hey buddy, I've gotta talk to Daddy about something. I want you to draw me a picture to hang on my wall, okay?"

"I'm done waiting for her, Ty. I can't do this to myself anymore. I've waited two years for her to realize it was okay to move on. The way we are together has felt like a real relationship minus the sex. I guess I just let myself believe it was more than what it really was."

"Dude, what the hell are you talking about?"

I looked at the screen saver on my phone. It was a picture of Claire and me on my birthday. She'd grabbed my phone and made me take a selfie with her. She was kissing my cheek and giving me bunny ears. It's one of my favorite pictures of us.

"She crushed me today, and she doesn't even know it yet. I wanted to give her everything she deserves. I had it all planned out in my head—marriage, another baby, growing old together. How could I have been so stupid?"

"Are you blind? What makes you think she doesn't want that from you?"

"I was driving past Gala's today and I saw her having lunch with Cole. I watched him kiss her on the cheek while holding her hand. She didn't see me drive by so she doesn't know I saw them. Why would she go back to him?"

"I saw firsthand the shit he put her through; she'd never take him back. There has to be an explanation. She's in love with you, and it scares the shit out of her. She's only loved one man the way she loves you, and she lost him. She thinks if she tells you how she feels and you reject her, then she'd not only lose you, but she'd lose Miles, too. Don't give up on her. Tell her how you feel."

"I feel like beating the hell out of him for touching her. I feel gutted picturing the smile on her face as he kissed her. I'm done, Ty; I'm over it." I stood and refilled my cup. "I met someone today, and she wants to hang out tonight. Her kid is in Miles' class, and she basically threw herself at me. I'm thinking a good hard fuck will ease my frustration."

"You stupid son of a bitch! If you screw my best friend over like that, I'll kill you myself."

Miles tossed the iPod and ran to the door. "Mommy!" He jumped into her arms.

"Hey there, love bug. How was school?"

"Good! Daddy's gonna go play with Adam's mommy later. Can I come to your house instead of Grandma's?

Her face turned white as a ghost. She looked at me with total confusion then her eyes watered up. I wasn't sure why she'd care; she had Cole. She put Miles down, and he hopped back up to his crayons.

"So you have a play date, huh?"

"It's nothing serious. I just met her today."

"It's none of my business, Gavin, and quite frankly, I don't want to hear about it, so please feel free not to share." She looked at Miles with warm, loving eyes. "As for Miles, I'm the only mother he has so, if he wants to come with me while you get your dick wet, then he can. I'm leaving at six so make your play date for after that." She gave Tyler a sad smile and walked out, her lip quivering.

I called Sasha and made plans for seven.

"Tyler, tell me I'm not an asshole."

"All I'm going to say is that if you do this, you'll lose her. Ask her about Cole before you throw away your future. Happily ever after or easy pussy, you decide."

****

The hot water from the shower poured down my back as I leaned my head on the cool tile wall. I couldn't get that look of hers out of my head, the pain in her big blue eyes and her beautiful lips quivering. What had I done?

I pulled into Claire's driveway, and before I could get out of the truck, she was helping Miles out. She looked at me with puffy eyes; I could tell she'd been crying.

"Just let him sleep here, I'm sure you'll be out past his bedtime, and I'll be taking him to school anyway. Oh, tell your sneaky bitch date not to be fake with me again or she'll regret it."

"What are you talking about?"

"Ask her about the dog park. It doesn't matter anyway. Wrap your shit up though, she's too easy to chance it."

"Claire, just let me ask you something."

"Bye, Gavin. Miles is waiting."

And just like that, she was walking away. Why was she so pissed off? This wouldn't bother her if she were back with Cole. I just messed it all up because of a girl I don't give a shit about. I needed to think, so I drove around the neighborhood for a few minutes and eventually ended up in Claire's driveway again. I had to tell her everything and ask about Cole. I walked up the front porch steps and heard them talking through the screen.

"I don't want a new mommy; I want you. I know I can call

you that, but I want you to be my real mommy, where you marry Daddy and live with us."

"Miles, it's not that easy. You'll understand when you get bigger. Daddy and I love each other very much, but it's different with us. He loves me like a best friend. I'm sure he's going to find someone who will love you very much, and you'll love her, too."

I could hear my son crying, and it was breaking my heart.

"Do you know what used to make my daughter feel better when she was sad? Music. I would play my guitar and sing to her. I haven't played my guitar in a very long time, but if you want me to, I'll play for you."

I can't believe I almost messed this up. She's my love, my son's protector, and I had to let her know how much I needed her.

"I'm going to play you a song that makes me think of your daddy, but it's got to be our secret."

I heard her take the guitar off the wall and call him to the floor with her. She strummed the guitar and began to sing. She had the voice of an angel.

I'm scared of falling; I'm scared of the pain
I'm scared of the rush that will course through my veins
With your skin on my skin, and your breath on my neck
If I had one wish, that's what I'd get
Someone please help me, I don't know what to do
I think that I've fallen, I've fallen for you
I think that I've fallen, I've fallen for you

I couldn't take it anymore. I rushed into the house and looked at Miles. "Go check on Calvin, buddy."

She dropped the guitar and backed up against the wall. I grabbed her beautiful face and leaned in to kiss her. Just as our lips were about to touch, she slapped me across the face...*hard.*

"What the hell, Claire?"

"Why are you even here? Where's Sasha?"

"I was on your porch the whole time, I never got her. I don't want her; I want you!"

"Do you have any idea what today is? You picked the day I needed you most to bail on me for some nasty little whore." She stormed away from me and sat on the couch. "Audrey would have been thirteen today. I should be throwing a big birthday party, and instead, I was putting flowers on her grave. The only time I feel at home is when I'm with you and Miles. I was going to ask you to stay with me tonight, but before I could, I was asked to babysit while you screwed someone else."

Her tears fell like rain.

"Claire I..."

"You hurt me, Gavin. I've been hurt by a man before, but this was different. You broke my heart today. What bothers me the most is that I have no right to be mad at you; we aren't even together."

"I saw you and Cole at Gala's. I thought you were back with him. I was hurt and angry, and that girl threw herself at me. She didn't even know my name. I'm so sorry, please."

"Fuck you, Gavin. Cole was at the cemetery when I got there. We went to lunch and talked about our daughter. You know the things he did to me. Do you really think I'd go back to him? I have more self-respect than to go back to the man who beat and raped me, no matter how much he's changed. You should have gone and gotten your frustration fuck, because if you think you can sweep me off my feet like a white knight after this, then you're crazy."

"I'm sorry, Claire! Please..."

"Go home, Gavin; I need to be alone. You can drop Miles off in the morning."

CHAPTER 5

Claire

I woke up and had to force myself out of bed. I'd cried myself to sleep after Gavin left, and my eyes totally gave it away. There was no way I was getting my contacts in today, and between the swelling and dark circles, makeup was a must. I was sure I'd see Sasha this morning, and I wondered what she'd say.

Call me childish, but I just had to look at her Facebook page. The girl is a stripper. I actually competed with a pretty, young, sexual acrobat and won. I had to laugh at the situation a little. I decided to let my inner nerd take the lead. I'd show her the girl he fell for. I pulled out the Hulk outfit Gavin bought me: a short, faded denim skirt, a purple tank top with Hulk on it, and Hulk converse. The outfit matched the tattoos of Hulk and She Hulk I have on my calves. I also put on my glasses with the green frames. I glanced at my reflection in the full-length mirror and smiled. I looked perfect.

I heard the door open and the TV turn on; Gavin must have used his key. I had no idea what I was going to say to him, but I couldn't hide from him forever.

"Claire, are you coming down?"

I headed to the kitchen with my heart racing; I could feel the pounding in my ears. I walked in, and he looked me up and down, smiling.

"Cute outfit! Did your boyfriend buy it for you?" Stepping in front of me, he handed me an iced coffee from Dunkin Donuts. "Can I interest you in a peace offering? It's blueberry, your favorite!"

"You're going to need a lot more than an iced coffee to get back into my good graces, Mr. Price. My boyfriend didn't buy me this, my asshole best friend did."

"Well then, he has good taste. He's a lucky bastard, too. It's not too often you find a girl who's hot as hell and can school you in the world of body art and comic books!"

"Stop kissing my ass. I'm still mad at you Gavin."

He looked me in the eyes, and with his adorable dimples showing, he flashed his million-dollar smile. I was losing myself in those bright blue eyes when he pulled me in for a hug. No matter how hard I tried to stay mad, I was defenseless against his sweet smelling Old Spice. I melted right into him.

"I'm sorry, Claire. I really fucked up. Can we just pretend yesterday never happened? I can't handle you being mad at me."

"Yeah, last night was hell. Today is a new day, and you're going to be late for work."

"Small price to pay for getting my baby girl back. I thought I'd lost you for good. I'd die without you, Claire." He kissed my forehead and rubbed his nose against mine.

I smiled at him and grabbed his chin. "Sweeter than a thousand!" I grabbed my purse and the stuff I'd need for the day and opened the door. "Let's go, love bug!"

I pulled into the school parking lot, and sure enough, Sasha was there waiting. Her shorts gave new meaning to the word *short,* and her tank top was so low-cut she was nearly falling out of it. I walked Miles in, and she followed behind us with her son. Carrie, the teacher's aide, saw me and waved. She was a regular at KC's, and I'd seen her at a bunch of comic trade shows. She was a total Marvel junkie.

"Hi, Mrs. Price. I'm loving the outfit, but I have to admit, I'm more of a Thor girl myself. How's the comic book store working out?"

I saw Sasha roll her eyes at the Mrs. Price comment.

"I'm not Mrs. Price yet, but I'm hoping for the job one day. The store is going great; I basically took the two stores and converted them into a bigger one with a bar-sized divider through most of the length. They both have their own entrance so you only need to be in both parts if you want to. You should really come check it out. Also, I need help for the comic side, so if you know of anybody, have them stop by."

"I'll definitely come check it out, and I'll ask around my circle of nerds about the job."

Sasha was outside waiting for me when I walked out. I wanted to smack that smug look right off her face, but deciding to be the better person, I walked right past her and headed for the car. I saw the boys' teacher sitting in her car with the windows down, gathering her things for class.

"Cute outfit if you're a thirteen-year-old tomboy. You can tell Gavin I missed him last night. He can call me if he wants to reschedule since you two are just friends."

"Oh, thanks. Gavin bought it for me. He loves that I prefer to have my personality showing and my lady parts covered. He didn't get you last night because he doesn't go for little girls who throw themselves at strangers." I smiled, both amused and proud of myself for speaking up. "You practically begged him to sleep with you, and you didn't even know his name. Have a little self-respect, girl. Did you think he wouldn't tell me? That's cute. Trust me, there's no need to reschedule; I've got all his needs covered."

"Whatever, loser."

"Yup, this loser is off to run both of her businesses. Have a nice day darlin'; I think I hear your pole calling you."

I turned and waved at the teacher with a rush of satisfaction. I headed to the shop wondering where Gavin and I stood now that things were pretty much out in the open. All I knew was I was happy our first fight was over.

Tyler didn't even let me out of the car before she pounced on me. "He told me you kissed and made up, well, made up anyway. Did you really bitch smack him?"

"He deserved it. We're all good though, and I told off that little skank at the school. I'll give you details later. I have to get my portfolio together for Saturday. I'm stealing some coffee to fuel my fire."

Both girls were working, so I brought coffee for all three of us.

"Thanks, boss lady!" Tara took the coffee from my hands.

She was gorgeous. Her shoulder length hair was always two colors, her natural black with something vibrant underneath and highlighted in; this week it was purple. She had a small hoop over the middle of her bottom lip and a diamond stud in her nose. She had lost a lot of weight recently, yet oddly enough, her breasts stayed the same size; usually that's what women loose first. Her body was a complete work of art, and Kayleb had put most of it there. Not only had she been his best friend, she'd also worked for him. As soon as I reopened the shop, she came right back. A lot of the regulars were really happy about that, because once a person is comfortable with a tattoo artist, they don't want to change it up. I loved this girl; if she weren't such a homebody, she would've been dubbed the fourth amigo.

"I'll take that!" Beth took her coffee and sat at her station.

Beth is a petite Italian girl with a black Mohawk and a New York accent. She seems intimidating at first, but she's really a quiet person—and a hell of a good artist. I've never spent time with her out of the shop, but Tara told me she's the drummer in a band.

I sat in the comic store surfing through pictures on my laptop from the Halloween party we threw last year that I could use. Devil's Night should be scary but fun at the same time so there were plenty that were fitting for the occasion. I had a few zombie pictures that were cool, a picture of a bunch of the guests dressed up and doing the "Thriller" dance, and picture of Tara tattooing a huge Frankenstein on someone's back. That picture was awesome. The angle of her face made it easy to see how into it she was. I could use these, but I needed something new, more dark and daring. Since that "Grey" book came out, BDSM had become the new craze, and now it was everywhere. I had to admit I was intrigued by it as well. The thought of erotic, sexual pleasure that could come from things you dared to try, and the fear of not knowing how much further your body would allow you to go. As long as I made them tasteful, I could take a few of those: dark and erotic not trashy and pornographic. What I needed was a model; I needed Tara.

I ran to her station to catch her before she left. "I need you to do me a huge favor, doll face."

"What's that?"

Staring into her big, green, doe eyes, I fluttered my eyelashes at her. "Model for me, Tara. Please? For the gallery expo. I meet with the owner on Saturday to show her my pictures, and I have a few dirty ideas I'd like you to bring to life."

"What? Claire, I'm not a model."

"But you could be. You have the perfect look for the type of alternative, erotic beauty that I want. You'll be my visual submissive, I'll turn that innocence of yours into some ink-filled kink."

"You're crazy, but let's give it a try. I want copies of them though. Every girl needs a few sexy pics of herself somewhere along the line."

"How would you feel about being tied up? Let's take this into the back so we don't draw in an audience. Anyway, I can duct tape your ankles to the chair and use my scarf to tie your hands behind your back. The sexual desire is all in your face and body language; the camera just freezes your moment. What are you willing to take off for me? Are you feeling brave?"

"What is it they say? 'Go big or Go home'. "

"I'm not sure who 'they' are, but tell them I said thanks."

There she was, sitting spread-eagle on a wooden chair, her ankles secured to the legs of the chair with duct tape over her combat boots. Her wrists were tied behind her back with a sheer, black scarf. All she had on was a black lace thong, matching bra, and a garter belt with purple fishnet stockings. Her tattooed arms and the scorpion tattoo under and around her navel looked perfect. Her facial piercings just added to the sex appeal. I grabbed my camera and got to work, shooting different angles and setting up different poses for her. I could tell she was enjoying herself, so I didn't feel bad for asking her to do it in the first place.

"Fifty Shades of Tara! Thank you so much. Next month's rent is on the house."

I noticed her blush and turned around. There was Gavin.

"Now ladies, why wasn't I invited to this party?"

Tara laughed at him while she dressed and smiled as she headed back to her station. "Because I prefer my boss' boyfriend not see my goodies."

"Fair enough." He gave me a seductive smile. "So I'm the boss' boyfriend now?"

Trying to ignore his statement, I flipped through the pictures. "I'm going to edit these tomorrow, and I have some from last year's party I want to use. What's this chick's name again?"

"Her name is Sarah Jenkins, and I'm sure she'll love what she sees." He pressed his body against me and grabbed my hand. Putting his lips to my ear, he whispered, "She'd love to see this, too"—his erect cock dug into my belly—"so don't tell her it's waiting to meet you"—he nuzzled his mouth into my neck and gently bit me—"soon."

Before I knew it, my hand was cupping his dick. My jaw dropped. He'd never been so physically forward before. My insides were melting; I wanted him to touch me, and I needed to touch him. Trying to catch my breath, I forced myself back to reality. "You're nasty!"

I laughed a little and then realized he'd already let go of my hand, and I was still holding onto him. I'm not sure why, but I decided to start stroking him. His head was tilted back, and with deep breaths, he hummed through his closed lips. I slowly unzipped his jeans, stuck my hand through his fly, and wrapped it around his thick shaft. I started to jerk him off, but stopped after a minute or so. I kissed his cheek and shook my head no.

"Oh, you little tease. If you didn't have customers out there,

I'd show you just how nasty I can be." Lifting my skirt up, he tore off my red satin thong with one tug and kissed it before he put it in his pocket. "Naughty girls wear red; I'd like to make you my naughty girl." He squeezed my ass and rubbed his face through my hair, breathing in the scent of my shampoo. "Oh, the things I'd love to do to you! These pictures are G-rated compared to the fun we could have." He dug his nails into my skin, and his voice deepened. "I will feel you from the inside, love. Eventually, my cock is gonna make you scream."

I closed my eyes and took a deep breath. I tried so hard not to pay attention to him and focus on anything else, but I just couldn't. His words, his voice, the firm, controlling grip on my ass were all so overwhelming. I felt my skin flush hot and red as he made my clit throb, my entire body tingle, and my knees weak. I let out a soft whimper.

"Oh my God, did I just make you cum, baby girl?" He pushed me against the counter and gave me a wicked smile as he ran his finger through my folds to feel my arousal. "The first time was an accident; this is on purpose." My hips bucked forward as his fingers circled my still throbbing clit. "Here's a little preview for us." Tightly wrapping his fist in my hair, he looked me straight in the eye as he pushed two fingers deep inside me, in and out, fast then slow, over and over without taking his eyes off mine. "You like that, don't you? I can tell you do, you're shaking. Next time I'm inside you, it's not gonna be my fingers, so get this tight little pussy ready because I don't play nice." I couldn't help it; I gripped the counter, moaning as I came again. He put his fingers in his mouth to taste me, and in a deep, sexy voice he whispered, "Mmm… so sweet. I see it's nice and smooth for me, too. I like that." He nipped my neck again while rubbing his erection over my wet pussy. "Do you see what you do to me? I want to fuck you so bad, nice and hard. I'm gonna have to go home and jerk off now." He pulled down my skirt and kissed my forehead. With a finger under my chin, he tilted my head up and smiled. "I'll have you soon."

And just like that, he turned and left.

CHAPTER 6

Claire

I sat in the back of Starbucks waiting to meet the woman who would decide whether my work was good enough for the Penne Visa Gallery. The place was beautiful, newly renovated and modernized for a younger crowd. I was hoping my cinnamon dolce latte would ease my nerves, but it didn't, not one bit. Even though I felt like a shaky mess, my inner diva was in full control, and I was dressed to impress. I had borrowed Tyler's knee-length, gray dress and yellow thigh highs for a pop of color. Her gray stilettos were killing me already—I just don't get how some women wear them all the time—and as nice as they look, I couldn't wait to get them off. I sent Gavin a text saying I'd let him know as soon as the meeting was over. Just as I put my phone down, Ms. Sarah Jenkins walked in. She grabbed a latte and a scone and joined me at my table.

"Hi, I'm Sarah, you must be Claire."

She was pretty in a hard sort of way, like Gillian Anderson in *The X-Files*. The dress suit and her hair in the tight bun made her look older than her years. I wondered if she really was into Gavin; it could work to my advantage if she was. I'd pictured her wanting a more clean-cut type, although I assumed she'd only seen him in his work clothes with his hair pulled back. His handsome face and intoxicating eyes could attract anyone, but I couldn't see her on the back of his Harley.

"So, Mr. Price said you work at a tattoo shop."

"Well, I own the tattoo shop and the adjoining comic book store. Photography is a hobby for me, always has been." I pulled out my portfolio to show her the pictures from the party and of Tara.

"I love this one." She pointed at one of the pictures from last year.

Two people from the party were dressed as zombies from the 50s. The girl had on a white halter-top and pink poodle skirt, and she wore victory rolls in her hair. The guy looked like a zombie greaser with his slicked back hair and leather jacket.

"It was taken at Ace's Diner. I bought them a milkshake, put two straws in it, and they let me photograph them in exchange for a copy of the picture."

"These are wonderful, too. She's very beautiful. Who is she?"

"My friend Tara. She's a tattoo artist at my shop."

"Each photographer is allowed to bring six pictures to present. Bring as many copies as you like as well as business cards. I hope you choose one of your friend; it's up to you though. I'd like to buy one of her for the gallery, so I'll be in touch about that. Remember, Devil's Night at 6 o'clock. I'll email you details. Congratulations, Ms. Michaels!"

"Thank you so much, Ms. Jenkins!"

I shot Gavin a text telling him to come meet me and went to get another latte. As I sat back, I tried to take it all in. This was so exciting. Not only were my pictures going to be part of a real expo, but it would be on Devil's Night. I couldn't think of a theme more fun to do, except comics of course. I was pulled out of my trance when the door opened and Detective Morgan Rice strolled in. Rice had been Cole's partner since Cole made Detective when Audrey was four. He's also Gavin's cousin. Even though he's eye candy at its finest, he's the most arrogant man I've ever met. He's a light-skinned black man with striking green eyes, and his body looks like it's straight out of a men's fitness magazine. I had to admit there were times I wanted to run my hands over his smooth shaved head, but Cole would have killed me. I've tried to steer clear of him because, ever since I left Cole, he's been trying to get me to sleep with him. He's not used to hearing the word *no* from the ladies, so I'm pretty sure he's taken it as a personal challenge to get me into bed. I thought about telling Cole, but that would end badly; one would be dead and the other in prison.

Once he spotted me, he came over to say hi. He leaned in for a hug, so I followed his lead, hugging him back and hating every second of it. Before I knew it, his hands were creeping up the back of my dress, his fingertips just slightly under the bottom of my panties. I'm not sure how much was visible to onlookers, but they'd seen my garter belt at the very least.

"Hey, my love, you look mighty fine today."

I felt nauseous, partially because I'd been violated in the middle of Starbucks and partially because he thought the badge on his belt told him he could.

"Get your hands off me! I am not, nor will I ever be 'your love', so give it up. If you touch me again, I'm not going to have to tell Cole what a scumbag his partner is; he'll know it when I rip your dick off and use it to stir my coffee."

I heard a chair move behind us and a voice said, "Dude sit down, it's not our business, and he's a cop. She's not hurt, so don't play hero." I couldn't even bring myself to turn around and see who was behind me; sheer embarrassment wouldn't allow it.

"Those are some big words from such a pretty little thing. You'll give it to me one day; they always do. My cousin might not be man enough to keep trying, but I, my dear, can be very persuasive."

I had to laugh because I noticed Gavin standing right behind him.

The only reason Gavin didn't get any was bad timing. I wasn't ready to move on. If he weren't my best friend, I'd have fucked him senseless by now; I still may.

Morgan noticed Gavin standing behind him and stormed off in a huff. "Well, Thanksgiving should be interesting this year."

"I'm in! I can display six pictures and bring as many copies as I want. She wants to buy one of Tara and keep it in the gallery. Gav, I can't even tell you how much this means to me. I'm thinking you should slip her some dick as a sign of gratitude, a special thank you for picking me."

"Either that, or we can discuss not being best friends anymore so you can fuck me senseless; I do believe those were your exact words. I'll even pick up the best friend title again afterwards."

"Don't you wish?" I scooped some whipped cream off my latte and slowly sucked it off my finger.

"You have no idea. Actually, I'm sure you do."

My phone rang; it was Tyler. She always had the knack of calling at the worst possible time.

"Hey, girl."

"So, are we celebrating tonight?"

"Yup, sure are. Holy shit, I have a crazy story for you."

"Cool, well, 9 o'clock at Brown's. Call Gavin and tell him to meet us."

"He's here with me. I'll tell him."

"I should have known he'd be locked to your hip since he's not at work."

"Goodbye, ass."

I ended the call and turned back to Gavin. "We're meeting at Brown's at 9 o'clock."

"No," he countered. "I'm picking you up for dinner at 6 o'clock. Let's have the Three Amigos be an amigo short for a little bit. It doesn't have to be a date, just some time for us." He kissed my forehead and said, "Sweeter than a thousand!"

I got in my car and called Tyler back to tell her everything, the meeting, Rice, and all that had happened with Gavin.

"Tyler, I just can't shake him. The man made me cum twice in the span of ten minutes, and he barely touched me."

"Holy shit! Enough is enough; just get on your knees already."

"I just might. Dinner is at 6 so come dress me at 5."

"I'll be there at 4:30 so we can do your hair. I want you looking irresistible"

"It's not a date, Ty. It's just dinner."

"If it was just dinner then I'd be invited. Gotta go, though. I'll see ya soon."

Tyler actually showed up on time with a tote bag full of God knows what and a bottle of wine.

"You pour, I'll go set out the clothes." I think she was almost as excited as I was.

I had the same butterflies I did when Tyler primped me for prom. We were each other's dates and had an absolute blast. Quite a few disappointed boys had asked her, but she wanted us to be the real life Romy and Michelle.

I poured our wine and headed up to my room for some girlie fun. She had my king size bed covered with a mix of my clothes and hers. There were so many outfits I wondered how she'd done it in the short time I was downstairs.

"Ty, I told you it's not a date, and I'm not getting all dressed up to go to Brown's after. Besides, he knows I'm not the princess type. I'm going as myself."

"How about a compromise? I'll pick the pants and shoes; you pick the shirt and hairstyle. I want you to wear my black leather pants with a tee shirt of your choice. Wear your biker boots with it and you'll look hot as hell."

I pulled out my red Mrs. Vincent Elliot shirt and leather cuffs. "Well?"

"Perfect! If Penny and Leonard from *The Big Bang Theory* had a daughter, it would be you!"

After I got dressed and did my makeup, she packed her bag up. "I'm taking your black corset top to wear and your black boots." She softly kissed my lips and smiled. "You really do look beautiful, Claire."

CHAPTER 7

Gavin

Why did I say it wasn't a date? What the hell was I thinking? I scolded myself the whole way to her house. *She let me put my fingers inside her; there's no way she'd turn down a dinner date. I just need her to take that damn ring off. Moving it isn't enough, I need it off completely.* When I got there, I went right in. I loved having the key to her house; it made it seem like we were a real couple.

"Where are you, baby girl?"

"I'm in the kitchen letting Calvin in."

I went to get her, and she was bent over petting him. Good God, what a sight. The top of her red lace thong was showing a little. I swear I wanted to rip it off and bend her over the kitchen table. It was getting a lot harder to control myself with her; I wasn't sure how much longer I could. She turned to me and smiled, and I had to act like I wasn't lost in my own dirty mind.

"Hey beautiful, I love those pants on you."

"Thanks! I was hoping you would."

"Oh, were you? It's nice to know you dress to impress me, although wearing no clothes would impress me even more." I kissed her forehead and pulled her in for a hug. "Where do you want to go for dinner? Your choice."

"How's Red Robin sound? I could use some beef in my life." She grabbed my hand and pulled me toward the door.

"Well then, lets skip dinner, I got your beef right here!" I pulled our hands down to my dick to make her laugh. I loved her beautiful smile.

"You're nasty! It does sound tempting, but if I get you into my bed, we aren't getting out. Let's go, lover boy!"

"Burgers it is!"

She loved those burgers with the pineapple on them; it's the only thing she orders when we come here. I watched her as she bit into her burger, and some of the sauce stayed at the corner of her lip. I couldn't help myself, and I wiped it away with my thumb and sucked it off. I felt a flutter in my stomach. It's the closest I've been to those luscious lips. Why does this girl make me feel like a lovesick teenager?

"I don't know whether to feel like a slob or blush."

"If we go with blush, then that means I'm doing something right."

After dinner, we had about an hour to kill so we went to the beach to talk. I drove the truck right up to the shoreline, and we hopped into the bed. It felt so right, just lying there under the starry sky. We joked around about the Sasha situation and talked about the expo a bit but ended up just lying there, her cuddled into my chest.

Looking at me with a sweet yet serious expression, she said, "Have you ever just stopped and paid attention to how beautiful the moon is? Everyone talks about or wishes on stars, but not many people talk about the moon."

"I guess I really haven't."

"I used to tell Audrey the moon was special because it was the one thing we could look at and know that, no matter how far away from each other we were, we would be looking at the same big, beautiful moon. She loved the moon." She lifted her head to look at me. "If I ever get to have another baby, maybe I'll name him or her Luna."

"After that song you love?"

"No, silly, *luna* is the Spanish word for moon."

All I could do was gaze into her big blue eyes and smile. She amazed me; every word she said made me love her more. I wanted to tell her how much I love her, but I promised myself I wouldn't until she took the ring off. A small tear ran down her cheek, and her beautiful pink lips started to quiver. I twirled some of her long hair around my finger and ran my thumb down her cheek, tracing the path of the tear. I knew she wanted me to kiss her; I could see it in her eyes, but I just couldn't.

"Time to go, baby girl, it's almost 9. Thanks for the one-on-one time. I liked having you all to myself."

"Anytime, I loved it! Just between us, I don't like the idea of sharing you with anyone."

CHAPTER 8

Claire

We pulled into Brown's, and I saw Tyler waiting outside looking as gorgeous as ever. Her size D breasts are bigger than mine usually, but in my corset, they were massive.

"Damn, she looks good!"

"Ahhh, is that why I got shot down? Did you switch teams on me?" His grin was evil and made those dimples I loved show. "Now, that's a show I'd love to watch!"

"No watching today, big boy. I'm just admiring the view tonight. My question is why didn't you try to scoop her up?"

"I'd be lying if I said I didn't think she's beautiful, but let's just say"—he slowly ran his hand up my thigh until his fingers squeezed between my legs—"my sights are set elsewhere. Lucky for me, I'm a very patient man. Let's go before she kicks my ass for making her wait."

Tyler came running up and slapped my ass hard. "Damn, you look good in my pants. I'm sure you look hotter out of them though." Her gaze crept up to Gavin's.

He stood between us. "Hey now, little lady, nobody's smackin' that but me!"

"I know I'm loved, but I'm going inside. You can fight over my ass in there!"

Dave saw us walk in. "Look who it is: My dynamic duo, Blondie and Little Miss Trouble!" He ran up and gave us our regular bear hug, and the barely legal blonde he had been sitting with gave us looks that could kill.

"Looks like your youngster is feeling a little left out, Dave." Ty laughed and waved at her.

"Stop Ty, you know the old man needs some young pussy before he can sleep at night."

Dave noticed Gavin with us and shook his hand. "I'm Dave, and I own this dump."

"I'm Gavin. I'm the guy responsible for turning your dynamic duo into the three amigos!"

"Well, in that case, Gavin, go get my girls their drinks and tell the bartender your stuff's on the house. I've got a young lady to tend to!"

We made our way to one of the round bar tables next to the jukebox. I knew the free play code so I intended to bring down the house tonight. First on the list was "Are You Gonna Be My Girl" by Jet. That song makes me and Tyler dance like fools even when we're sober, so what better way to start the fun?

Gavin came back with round one. "Coronas for my queens!"

"Thanks, homie!" Tyler grabbed her beer and started singing to me as if the bottle was a microphone.

"Thank you, my king." I blew him a kiss and winked

My fingers grazed his hand as I took the bottle. I looked him straight in the eyes as I drank my beer, giving flirty smiles between sips. I had the power; I'd make him mine. He stepped closer and pressed me against the table. As his soft hair grazed my cheek, my heart began to race, goosebumps ran up my arms, and my legs turned shaky and weak. This man was my kryptonite.

He whispered in my ear, "I'm not sure where you're going with all the extra flirting, baby girl, but if your goal is to make me hard, it's working."

Softly biting my neck, he rubbed his erection over my hip just enough for me to know it was there. He gave me a small peck on the cheek and stepped back. I was so frustrated; I was supposed to be the tease. His phone rang, and I couldn't take my eyes off his perfect ass when he stepped outside to talk.

"What the hell did I just see?" Tyler's gaze alternated between me and the door. "Just fuck him already. Save the lovemaking for round two because you need it rough and dirty the first time." She leaned against the jukebox, pointing and laughing at me. "You're so wet right now that even *I* can feel it."

Just then, I heard a familiar voice behind me, but I couldn't place it. "I like your shirt."

"Sorry buddy, but that line is reserved for girls with titties popping out." I started to turn around. "I'm not inter—" Words escaped me when I saw him, my TV husband, the one and only Winston Ryan, and man, did he look good.

"I was wondering if I could buy my wife"—he pointed at my shirt—"and her incredibly sexy friend a drink."

Tyler blushed, and she was speechless. In twenty years of friendship, I've never once seen Tyler speechless. She liked him more than I did. She was all about the show, but I'm pretty sure she only watched it because of him. His co-star, Dylan Cross, was cuter. They did a good job making Dylan look like a bad boy for the show, but in all the off-screen pictures I've seen since he shaved of his beard three seasons ago, he had more of a pretty boy look.

"Do you lovely ladies have names?"

"I'm Claire, and my slightly star-struck friend over there is Tyler."

"It's nice to meet you. Tyler, I have to say it's a good thing that you're the one who struck my fancy because I'm very fond of my dick, and word on the street is that Claire likes to use them to stir her coffee." He stepped closer to Tyler. "Would I be out of line if I said I'd like to make you very fond of it as well?"

"Um, maybe, but I'm not going to fall on my knees just because you ask me to. You need to try a little harder if you want me."

"Well then, I love a good challenge. Can I at least get you ladies to go trade shirts? I'm enjoying the view in that one but I'd love to see my name spread across those beauties."

I hated to break up the steamy conversation, but I couldn't help it. "Wait, were you in the coffee shop today? Was it you who almost said something?"

"No, that was Dylan; I was the asshole who made him sit down. We can't get in trouble with the law, and it seemed like that's exactly what would have happened. You seemed to have it under control anyway; he ran off with his tail between his legs."

"Dylan, as in Dylan Cross? Like Aaron Dean, President of Brothers of Mayhem?" I realized how overly excited I must have seemed because even Tyler laughed at me. "I just sounded like a teenage fangirl, didn't I?"

There he was, walking up to us with his hands full of beer.

His thick, black hair was gelled into a spiky mess. His sharp jawline made the defined cleft in his chin more noticeable, and he had the most awkward smile. "Hi, I'm Dylan. We were hoping to make a few new friends. Do you mind if we join you?"

"Not at all. I'm Claire and this is Tyler."

"I saw a guy with you so I grabbed five beers. Did he leave?"

I felt Gavin squeeze my hips and push his body against me, like he was claiming me. Call me crazy, but him being so territorial was such a turn-on.

"No, I'm right here. He turned to me and smiled. "That was the babysitter. Miles is sick, but my Mom is going to go stay at my house tonight so I don't have to leave. I told her I was with you, and I didn't even have to ask."

"What can I say? She loves me!"

Tyler chimed in. "Winston wants me and Claire to switch shirts so he can claim my rack." She grabbed his beard and made him face her. "If he plays his cards right, he may end up claiming a lot more before the night is over."

"I see, so is Mr. Cross trying to snap you up?" I could see the jealousy burning in his eyes."

"As gorgeous as she is, I'm a married man. I also get the impression she's taken."

"I'm not taken by anyone… *yet*!"

Gavin ran his fingers down my cheek and kissed the tip of my nose. "Go trade shirts then meet me outside. We need to talk about this...us."

Tyler grabbed my hand and looked at Winston. "Five

minutes and I'm all yours!"

We hurried off to the bathroom as requested. Was this really happening? Had today really happened? I was on cloud nine. Not only did I get into this awesome expo, but I was hanging out with two of my favorite celebrities. Not to mention, I would probably leave here as Gavin's girlfriend.

"Claire, tell me I'm not a whore. We both know this isn't my style at all. What would you do if you were me? Be honest with me."

"Dude, it's Winston Ryan. If I wasn't crazy in love with Gavin, I'd be begging you to share. Get some dick and tell me all about it in the morning!"

I walked out the front door of Brown's just in time to see a woman with her back to me leaning into Gavin and running her fingers through his hair. I felt a huge pit form in my stomach, and I instantly needed to throw up. Then I saw him push her off him. My excitement turned to anger, and the hurt turned to fury. She turned around, and all I saw was black. It was Lark. The beautiful Lark, Cole's mistress. I hated her for her ugly soul but had to admit she was gorgeous on the outside. Her flawless, caramel-colored skin, perfect blonde curls, and emerald green eyes gave her the most exotic look I'd ever seen.

"Hey lover, long time no see. I saw you and figured I'd introduce myself to your new arm candy." She glanced at Gavin. "I thought about taking a ride on the last one, but rocker boy tattoo artists aren't my thing. This one, on the other hand, is very pretty. It might take some work, but I'm sure I'll have him on his knees, too. I'll even let you watch...for old times' sake."

She knew how to get under my skin and did a damn good job of it. Once I left Cole, he dropped her like a hot potato thinking it would make me come back. She must have really loved him in her own twisted way because she still held a grudge all these years later.

My blood was boiling, and I felt myself turning into a different person, one I never knew existed. "Bitch, if you're smart, you'll back the fuck up right now. Walk away before I beat your ass to the ground."

"Says the little one who curls up and cries. I've watched you crumble; I'm not afraid of you one bit."

Gavin ran in to get Tyler, I assumed, to try and stop a fight that was obviously coming. I stepped up to her, face-to-face, my shaky fists clenched tight. Ty and Gavin stood there watching. I've never been quite sure why they didn't break it up. I'm not a fighter, so this rush of adrenaline was all new to me; I couldn't control it.

"You knew a different me, a weak and battered wife. I was never afraid of you; I was afraid of Cole. So my question is: Princess, do you really miss the taste of my pussy so bad that you'll try and suck off every man I'm with, or are you just a bitter whore? Either way, you're pathetic."

I saw her pull back her fist to swing so I stepped back, grabbed her by the hair, and planted my fist into her face...twice. I think I broke her nose because blood gushed everywhere and mixed with her tears. It was such a rush to know I had it in me, that I could put her in her place. I felt Tyler pull me off her and start dragging me to the truck. "You want more?" I called out. "Come find me, bitch." Tyler threw me into Gavin's truck and slammed the door.

I watched Tyler give Winston a kiss on the cheek and smile. She shrugged her shoulders. I heard her even through the closed window. "I'm sorry; that bitch had it coming, though. I'm actually kind of proud of Claire for finally standing up to her. If you guys want to follow us to her house that would be awesome, but if not, I totally understand. Either way, it was amazing to meet you. Who would have thought my TV crush would be so awesome in real life...and think I'm hot!"

Winston gave her a smile. "Well you're all mine tonight so I guess we're coming. Lead the way, gorgeous."

On the way home, nothing was said, and I just stared at my bloody hands. I could tell Gavin was pissed off, but I didn't regret it, no matter how childish it was. At my house, he flopped on the couch, and I went upstairs to clean up. I was so tired of trying to impress him, trying to seduce him, and all the back and forth. After washing my face and hands, I looked in the mirror and took a deep breath. I slipped on some sweats and a tank top. It was time to get back to the basics, back to being me. By the time I got downstairs, everyone was sitting there talking. God only knows what was going through Dylan's and Winston's head. They all looked up, and I couldn't hold my tongue anymore.

"Gavin, I can't do this anymore, all the flirty games we play. They're fun, but this whole situation is driving me crazy. Look at us; we're a goddamn Taylor Swift song waiting to be written. That girl fucked my husband for years, and I did nothing. Tonight, I broke her nose just for touching your hair. What do I need to do to show you that I want you, that you're the one? What's it going to take for you to want me?"

"Claire it's not that simple."

"Why not? Why won't you be straight with me? I was damn near naked in bed with you the other night, and all you did was say goodnight; then earlier you pull what you did in the back of my shop, and tonight you're back to not wanting me. Am I too late? Is there someone else that you don't want to tell me about?"

"*Someone else?* Are you insane? I haven't touched another woman since the day I met you. I've been waiting all this time for you to be ready. For the last two years, I've been competing with a goddamn ghost, Claire. Do you have any idea how frustrating that is? I'm not giving you all of me until I know that I have *all* of you." He raked his hands through his hair trying to calm down. "You left Cole; you took your daughter and left. Kayleb died saving your life, trying to save Audrey's. If that accident hadn't happened, we'd have never met, and you'd be married to him."

"I'm ready; I've been ready. Why won't you believe me? I've been in love with you for so long and felt guilty for it. Guilt was the only thing holding me back. Well, fuck guilt; I love you. I love you, and I love Miles."

He lowered his voice. "Then why do you still wear his ring? You should be wearing my ring. I want to spend the rest of my life with you. I want you to adopt Miles so we can be a real family, but I need to know I'm the only one in your heart. I won't share my wife with anyone, alive or dead."

It all made sense now, I hadn't even thought of that. Why was I still wearing it anyway? I took it off and tossed it to Tyler. We stood in silence staring at one another until I couldn't take the silence any longer.

"What are you waiting for?"

CHAPTER 9

Gavin

Her words were spinning through my mind. Were they real, or was I dreaming? It was time; she belonged to me now. I charged toward her, pinning her to the wall, and I leaned in to kiss her. She grabbed the back of my head and returned my kiss, almost violently. Finally getting to kiss her was the fiercest and most passionate moment I'd ever experienced. The way our tongues danced together in perfect harmony sent chills down my spine. It was as if our mouths were made solely for one another's kiss.

This woman is my life.

"Take my girl upstairs and give her what she's been waiting for."

"Yes, ma'am, we'll see you all in the morning. We've got some work to do."

I threw her over my shoulder, carried her up to the bedroom, and smacked her ass on the way up the stairs. We stood at the foot of the bed just looking at one another. I had waited so long for this moment not knowing if it would ever come.

She is the only woman who has ever made me want to be what I know I need to be, made me desire a normal life. How did I manage to get her to fall in love with me? This once-unattainable beauty was finally mine.

"I want to undress you." I gently pushed her sweatpants

down over her hips and let them fall to the floor. Slowly running my fingers up her body, I pulled her shirt over her head, exposing her beautiful, bare breasts. Smiling at her, all I could say was, "You're perfect."

I fell to my knees and worshipped her. I gently kissed the inside of her thighs up to her lace panties, already wet with her arousal. I pulled them down with my teeth as I slowly rubbed and circled her clit. Her whole body was trembling, whimpers and moans coming from that beautiful mouth, and I had barely touched her.

"Your pussy is so beautiful, so soft, and wet already." I stroked along her cleft before sliding inside of her. "You're so tight; I love it. I can't wait to open you up."

Her heavy breathing fueled my need to be inside her.

"Is this really happening?"

"It's happening, baby girl. Are you ready for me to take what's mine?"

"Yes, I'm all yours."

I ran my tongue inside the folds of her pussy and gently nipped at the lips, claiming my prize. Softly fluttering my tongue over her clit, as my fingers sank deep inside her, triggered a shattering moan that was music to my ears. She was my instrument to play, and I would play her well. The beautiful sounds she made as I touched her were driving me wild, and her taste was now my sweet addiction. She grabbed my hair, yanked my head back, and looked into my eyes.

"Please, Gavin, make love to me. I need you."

We moved to the bed, and I became lost in the sight of her beautiful face as she reached to undo my belt buckle. I gave her a devilish smile as she tugged down my pants. Her eyes widened at the sight of my erection.

"I told you, he's my *not-so-little* friend."

"Well, now, he's all mine to play with." She gave me a bad girl look full of lust and want as she spread her legs to make room for me to move in between them. "I've been waiting so long for this Gav, I need you inside me."

Reality and responsibility struck. "I don't have a condom, and I didn't think this would really happen. I know you're clean, but…"

"Did you mean what you said? Do you want me forever?"

"Of course I did, Claire. I'd marry you tomorrow."

She smiled at me and cupped my face in her hands. "Let's make a baby!"

"Good God, I love you!"

Part of me wanted to take it slow, to softly make love to the woman I adored, but as our bodies moved together, I became lost in the intensity of the moment. So many feelings swept through me, a mix of shaky, savage, and greedy. I could see the pleasure in her eyes as I claimed her. Pounding inside of her over and over, I lifted her long legs up so I could fill her completely.

"Your pussy feels so good, baby girl. I knew it would. It's all mine now."

Her back arched as she came, pressing her chest up to my mouth. My tongue circled her perfect pink nipples, so beautifully erect. I pinched and pulled them as I gently bit into the fullness of her breasts.

"I need your big cock, Gav, fuck me harder. Don't hold

back."

I drilled into her, balls-deep, making her scream. Using my last shred of self-control, I held out until I felt her pussy clench my dick as her entire body shook. I plunged in deep, with a hard, final thrust as I shot my load into her. Yelling my name, she exploded underneath me again.

We clung together in the midst of orgasmic fireworks. I could finally hold her as I said the words. "I love you, Claire."

Catching her breath, she sank deeper into my chest. "I love you, Gavin."

I waited until I knew she was asleep, and I went downstairs to see if Tyler was awake. Dylan was passed out on the couch so I figured she was upstairs with Winston. I saw her purse laying on the floor, so I grabbed it to find the ring I'd bought for Claire. I had seen it two months ago and fell in love with it. It was a white gold ring with a large, cushion cut, pale green diamond, surrounded by purple diamonds. I remembered Claire saying that she saw a line of jewelry based on Marvel characters and how cool it was. This ring reminded me of Hulk so I knew Claire would love it. I knew I'd eventually ask her to marry me so I had to buy it. I made Ty promise to keep it in her purse until I was ready to take it from her; sure enough it was there.

When I woke up, Claire was cuddled into the covers with her back to me. I pulled the ring from the side table and placed little butterfly kisses down her neck and shoulder to wake her up.

"Good morning, my love!"

I pulled her hips as close to me as possible and slid myself inside her. Slowly and lovingly our bodies became one. Breathing deeply we found our slow and steady rhythm, and I knew it was time. Pressing her against me, skin-on-skin, I put my lips to her ear.

"I can't wait to call you my wife."

I slid the ring onto her finger before intertwining her fingers with mine, clenching our grip. Moving together in a calming and powerful force, together we quietly found our release. We lay there, with my arms wrapped tightly around her, for what seemed like hours, lost in one another.

She was smiling, gazing at her ring. "It's so beautiful, Gavin. When did you get it?"

"Two months ago. It's been in Ty's purse the whole time. I knew I'd give it to you; I just didn't know when. I told you I wanted forever. You're my queen, baby girl."

CHAPTER 10

Claire

It was real; I couldn't believe it. I adored that beautiful ring on my finger. It was me in every way. I could lie here in his arms forever, but I just needed to show Tyler how it looked on me. There was a knock at the door, and it opened just a little.

"Hey guys, Tyler is making breakfast and wanted me to come get you." Dylan's face looked so uncomfortable, and I realized we were completely naked. "Oh shit, I'm so sorry!"

"Thanks!" I laughed and pulled the cover over myself.

I threw some sweats on and headed for the door, but Gavin pulled me back into him. He gave me a small peck on the lips. "I love my son more than life itself, but he wasn't planned. My ex and I weren't even a couple when she got pregnant. He's the reason I married her, I thought we could make it work." He kissed my forehead. "Was last night a let's-see-what-happens-in-the-heat-of-the-moment, or are we going to keep trying to get pregnant?"

"I was being serious, very serious. I want to be a mother again. I have Miles, and I want to adopt him, but I really want a baby. I really want *your* baby. I hope you feel the same way."

"I do, but I'd like us to be married before we have a child. I want to do it all the right way with you. I'm not saying I don't want to keep trying, I'm saying let's get married soon. Something small then I can go buck wild on you until there's a tiny version of us inside you!"

"How about a backyard barbecue wedding, small gathering of close friends and family? How does next weekend sound?"

"It sounds like I can keep filling you up regularly!"

"You're so romantic!"

He shoved my bottoms down and picked me up. I wrapped my legs around him as he pressed me against the door. His scent alone was driving me wild, a mix of his sweat and our sex made my body long to be filled. Tightly gripping my ass, he was deep inside me with one hard thrust. My body felt so full, so possessed. Wrapping my arms around his neck, I smiled at him.

"Just stand there and hold me. I'll take good care of you!"

I ran my fingers through his hair, still sweaty from my glorious wake-up call. I used my hips to slowly move my body up and down the long length of his cock at a steady and seductive pace. Pulling his hair so his head flew back, I softly kissed his lips.

"Let me suck your tongue."

The more I sucked, the harder he became. As he stretched me deep inside, I moved faster, grinding and bouncing until I couldn't take it anymore. My clit was swollen and throbbing as my insides pulsed and pounded.

His lips grazed my ear. "I meant what I said; you belong to me now." He sank his teeth deep into my breast causing a rush of pain that turned into an unfamiliar type of pleasure as his mouth pulled on it. I drug my nails down his back as I circled my clenched pussy around his rock-hard dick, milking every drop of cum he had as I exploded on top of him. When he put me down, I could feel his warm seed running down my thigh; it was such a rush knowing we could be so primal.

Catching my breath, I whispered, "Yes, I belong to you."

I heard Tyler yell from the bottom of the steps. "These pancakes aren't going to eat themselves, you know. You can eat now and suck his dick later."

We went to the kitchen and joined everyone for breakfast. Ty makes the best blueberry pancakes, and I was happy to see them waiting next to a huge plate of bacon. "What got into you Ty?"

Dylan laughed and pointed at Winston. "He did!"

"Oh, zip it!" She laughed along with him. "I know this is your favorite, so I made them to celebrate. Now, show me the ring already!"

"How did you know he gave it to me?"

"My purse wasn't where I left it. I've been carrying that thing around for the last two months and was forbidden to even look at it. Let me see it already!"

I held it up for everyone to see and she started to cry. "It's so beautiful, Claire. It's so *you*!"

"We aren't waiting. We don't want anything big, just a small backyard barbecue. Next Saturday is the plan, so make sure your store is covered."

"Wow, that's cool. It figures you'd go low key. It sounds like fun. You better wear a wedding dress though."

"Of course I will, and you and Tara are going to be right next to me. I said small, not plain." She tackled me, squealing like a schoolgirl. "Gav, can we have your mom do the ceremony? Didn't she do that online thing so she could do your Aunt Maggie's wedding?"

"Yeah, she did. She's going to cry her eyes out when I ask her. She loves you so much. She told me if I let you go, she'd kill me."

Gavin cleared the table and kissed my cheek. "Let me know what you need me to do. I suck at the whole planning thing."

Sitting with Tyler, we made small talk while Gavin cleaned up the kitchen. "Ty, I can't believe all this is real." I thought about the night before. "I can't believe I beat that bitch down. There was blood everywhere."

"She had it coming. I'm proud of you. Honestly, I didn't think you had it in you. It's good to see I'm finally rubbing off on you; it only took twenty years." She looked at Winston. "Hey lover boy, do you have plans next Saturday? I need a date to my best friend's wedding."

"Sounds like fun." He kissed my hand. "Congratulations Claire. Make a list of food and drinks you want there, and Dylan and I will make it happen. I know a few good barbecue spots in LA if you want to have it catered."

"Oh, I can't let you do that."

Dylan chimed in. "Call it a wedding gift. He's Tyler's date though. We aren't always a package deal. You don't have to invite me just because he's going."

"It would be cool if you came. Bring your wife."

"Well, the thing is, I was hoping you had a friend you could introduce me to so I'm not rolling fifth wheel. I'm only married on paper. We split over a year ago. I filed, but the divorce isn't finalized yet. My wife currently lives is San Francisco with her fifty-year-old sugar daddy. I said I was married because Gavin looked like he was going to slit my throat for checking you out."

Gavin came out of the kitchen and sat down by me. "I knew you were checking out her ass. It's all good. It's too nice not to notice."

Tara popped into my head, but she's kind of an introvert so I wasn't sure she'd even want a date, but considering it's in my backyard, she might go with it. "Well, my friend Tara is single. She's very pretty if you like the alternative type of girl." I showed him a picture of her. "If you like your girls decorated then I'll introduce you."

"Jesus, she's gorgeous. Hook it up, girl!"

"I'll be in my shop all day tomorrow. Stop in around 11 o'clock."

"Sweet! I'm really glad we decided on the small town Starbucks yesterday, you guys are awesome."

CHAPTER 11

Claire

"Good morning, sweetness!" I gave Tara her latte, handing it to her with my left hand. Her jaw hit the ground, and she jumped up, almost spilling the hot drink down the front of her shirt.

"Please tell me that's what I think it is! It's about damn time. I'm so happy for you!"

"Thanks! We decided we want to do it soon, a small intimate thing. A barbecue with a bonfire, music, friends, and fun. Then my husband can take me home and knock me up!"

"Sounds like a blast. So are you gonna name the baby Tara?"

"I make no promises. We are doing it next Saturday so you need to reschedule your appointments. I also need you to escort a friend of mine there."

"Who? If it's small and intimate, who's going to be there that I don't know?"

"He's a new friend. We actually just met this weekend. He's super sweet and incredibly easy on the eyes. Tyler is bringing his best friend. I told him to swing by at 11 o'clock to meet you."

"Come on, Claire, you know I don't do blind dates." I could tell she was pissed off at me. "The last two blind dates I went on were horrible. The first one ended with me finding out that he had a wife and a girlfriend because the wife stormed into the restaurant thinking I was the girlfriend. I had to use the mace I keep in my purse on the other one. Sorry girl, I swore myself off blind dates."

"It's not a blind date if you meet him first. Trust me, you'll love me for this."

The door opened and Dylan walked in. "Hi I'm—"

Tara interrupted, "You're Dylan Cross!"

He smiled at her. "Well, I was gonna say early, but that works, too."

"Huh?" She looked at me with wide eyes. "No fuckin' way!"

Dylan laughed. "So, is that a yes?"

She blushed. "Umm… I..."

"How about I take you out for dinner tonight, so we get to know each other before our first date?" He gave her his lady killer smile that so many girls got all wet in the panties over. "Except that would make tonight our first date."

"Are you sure? I mean, I'd love to but..."

He covered her lips with his finger. "You know, you're even prettier in person." He wrote down his phone number and rubbed his thumb across her cheek. "Call me when you get done work, and I'll come pick you up." He gave her a quick peck on the lips. "Later, beautiful."

Tara looked at me with the biggest grin on her face. "You are by far the coolest, Claire. I can't believe he called me beautiful. Dylan Cross thinks I'm beautiful. This has to be a dream."

I had to laugh at the look on her face. "I thought you didn't do blind dates."

"I thought it wasn't a blind date if I saw him first!"

"Tyler's going with Winston Ryan." I still couldn't believe it myself.

"How did all this happen?"

"It's a long story, I'll fill you in over lunch."

She sat in her chair, sipping her latte, still grinning from ear to ear. "Okay, back to earth. There was a message confirming the sign delivery today. Actually, they'll be here soon. Also, this envelope was under the door when I opened this morning."

I opened the envelope, and it was a picture of Gavin and me at Comic Con a few months ago. There was nothing written on it to let me know who'd left it or why. We were talking to one of the comic book artists about my shop. He was actually a really cool guy. He gave me shit about only having Hulk and Black Widow tattoos. He said if he ever saw me again I better have an Iron Man or Thor tattoo. I told him if he would do a promotional appearance at my shop, I'd get Iron Man tattooed anywhere he wanted, within reason. He told me to get it on my ass cheek so I could tell people that I got to sit on Robert Downey, Jr.'s face. Gavin didn't appreciate the comment; I, on the other hand, found it hilarious.

"This is creepy. I hope I'm not about to become a *Criminal Minds* episode." I sent Gavin a text telling him about it. I watched too much TV to not be worried.

The bell on the door to KC's chimed and in walked a very pretty woman. She had a short, chestnut colored bob, a petite frame, long legs, and gorgeous blue eyes that looked strangely familiar to me. Tara greeted her, but the whole time they were talking, she kept peeking into the comic shop at me. I smiled politely and waved even though she was creeping me out. Glancing at the clock, I realized it was already 2:30.

"I'm gonna go meet Gavin at the school. I'll be back soon." I gave the customer a nod as I left.

Gavin was standing outside of the school with the other parents, playing on his phone. I snuck up behind him and grabbed his waist, nuzzling my head in between his shoulder blades.

"Hey beautiful! How was your day?" He pulled me close and gave me a soft peck on the lips.

"Better now. I missed you."

I felt Sasha's eyes burn the back of my head. As juvenile as it may be, showing off the fact that he chose me felt so good. I showed him the picture from under the door, and he was just as confused as I was.

"I don't know what to say about it. Should we go to the cops? They can't really do anything with just a picture. We can just keep an eye out for anything strange."

"Okay. Just tell the lineup of ladies that you're officially off the market." I made sure I was talking loud enough for Sasha to hear. "I can't have a chick go all crazy, and I can't throw down once I'm pregnant."

"You're all I've ever needed, baby girl. You better know that by now."

"We have to decide who we want at the wedding so I can invite them. Why don't you guys stay at my place tonight, and we can figure it out?"

"We can do that and start packing your stuff to come move in with us, then you can hop on my baby maker."

"You're an ass." My phone started to buzz; it was a text from Tara. The sign had been put up for the comic store. I didn't tell anyone what the official name on the sign was going to be, I wanted it to be a surprise when they saw it.

"Mommy, Daddy!" Miles hopped up into my arms.

"I have a surprise for you back at the shop, love bug. You guys are both gonna love it!"

We drove back to the shop, and sure enough, there was the sign. It was a big white circle with a cartoon version of Miles wearing a Superman suit. The official name on it was **MILES OF COMICS**.

"Oh, my God, that's amazing, Claire!" Gavin was actually getting choked up. "So how do you like it, Mr. Monster?"

"Mommy, I'm Superman!"

CHAPTER 12

Claire

  I dragged Tyler with me to pick out a dress. I wanted something simple but pretty, obviously a wedding dress. We walked through Greyson's boutique and looked at so many different things, but nothing struck my fancy. We turned to leave and there it was. It was a 50s style, Audrey Hepburn-type dress, and I could picture how perfect it would look on me with a red flower in my hair. Simple and sweet, just like the wedding, I was in love with it.

  Tyler grabbed my hand and pulled me against her chest. "You are gonna look so pretty. I'm so glad this is finally happening for you guys." Wiping a tear away, she sniffled, "I love you both so much."

  "I love you, too. This wouldn't be happening if it wasn't for your wonderful match making abilities."

  Tara looked at me with an expression I wasn't sure how to read. "Claire, it's beautiful, but I…I need to go. I'm sorry, hun, for bailing on the wedding shopping for today. Call me later tonight, and we can talk."

  Tyler was pissed. "What the hell?"

  "It's okay. I'm not mad at all. I actually give her credit for leaving instead of bringing me down."

  "Credit? She just bails while we were supposed to be focusing on you. I'm so annoyed right now; I can't wait to tell her exactly what I think."

"Think about it Ty. She was Kayleb's best friend. All this would have been done for Kayleb and me. She's going to be fine. I'll call her later."

"I didn't think about that. I guess I get it. Enough about that, let's find a dress for me!"

We looked in a few different places and finally found the perfect dress for her. It was so nice, like the infamous white dress Marilyn Monroe wore in *Some Like It Hot* but it was red. They had Tara's size, too. "Tyler, in less than two weeks I'm going to be Mrs. Gavin Price! Can you believe it? Not to mention, my love bug is really going to be mine. I'm a mom again."

"Claire, he's been yours for a long time now, at least in his eyes. The only difference is, now you'll have the same last name."

"Let's call it a day, girl. I want to go home and see my future husband."

On the way home, I brought up the conversation Gavin and I had after I took the pictures of Tara. All he said and did that night had been running through my mind for the past few days.

"I thought the pictures were sexy and dangerous. If they were G-rated, what does he want to do to me? Is it weird that I want to know how kinky he wanted to be that night? He never did say anything even close to that again. He's a biter, but that's all he's ever tried. Our sex is amazing, but I want him to have exactly what he wants."

"Well, it looks like I'm taking my nephew for the night. I want you to show up after I pick up Miles and work your magic. You can use that power you have over him to get him to tell you exactly what he wants. Dress sexy, be seductive, and he'll be like melted butter!"

After I got home, I decided to take Calvin to the dog park until I knew Miles was with Ty. I needed some time to think after Tara ditched us. The very last thing I wanted to do was doubt Gavin and me. This was right; it was what I wanted and needed. Nothing was going to stop the happiness I felt with him. I threw the ball for Calvin to fetch a few times and noticed a woman staring at me; it creeped me out until I recognized her. She was the lady from the comic store a few days ago. She gave me a fake smile when she realized I noticed her. I had an awkward feeling in my gut. Something told me she had potential to be a royal bitch.

She walked over to me. "Hi, I'm Sammie. I recognize you from the tattoo shop."

"Yeah, that was me. I own the shop. Did you book an appointment with Tara?"

"Yes. I'm coming in this week so she can add to the tattoo I have already."

"Tara's great at what she does, so I'm sure you'll love it. Oh, by the way, I'm Claire."

"I know your name already; Duke and I have to split." She pet her dog then shook my hand.

Maybe I was wrong. She seemed nice enough, a little rough around the edges, but nice nonetheless. I walked Calvin home and sent Gavin a text saying I'd be there soon.

Standing in the shower, I tossed around whether or not I wanted to explore uncharted territory. Was I making what he said out to be more than it really was? I had read enough books with all the BDSM in it and knew it was kind of different. Gavin didn't seem like the type to be into the whole pain room kind of thing. I also don't see him as the dominant type. There was something in his voice that day though, the power behind his words, that let me know there was a hidden desire. I needed to figure out what it was.

I decided to take Ty's advice and use sex appeal to get what I wanted. He loves when I wear red, so I chose my new red ribbon g-string. It's totally see-through in the front and ties together in a satin bow in the back; I knew he'd love it. The rest of the clothes seemed pointless. I threw on my makeup, put on my leather coat and left. I was off to please my lover.

I walked into his house, and he was sitting on the couch. He looked me up and down with a huge smile on his face. "Mmm… now what have we here? I'm curious, my little minx, what are you wearing under that jacket?"

"We need to talk about something."

"No, we can talk later. Right now, I need to eat that delectable pussy."

Letting the coat fall to the floor, I climbed on his lap and straddled him. Pushing my breasts into his face, I ran my fingers through his hair and whispered in his ear. "I want to give you a little extra fun tonight, big boy. I want you to do anything you want with me."

Biting and pulling at my nipples, his eyes met mine. "Where is all this coming from? You do give me everything want."

I started to slowly grind on him. "I was thinking about the very first time you made me cum. You said you'd show me how nasty you could be, how much fun you could have with me. If those kinky pictures were G-rated, then I want to know what your version of NC17 is."

"Baby girl, I love our sex life; I don't want to hurt you. I've pushed away some hard-core desires; I just lost control that night. I shouldn't have said those things. I'm sure you've picked up on how much I love to bite you, to claim you as mine. Isn't that rough enough for you?"

"Normally, yes, I love the way we make love. It's just that I know you want more; I can see it in your eyes. I want one night of hard-core fucking; do anything to me you want. Dominate me; own me. I promise I'm not going to say no to you. I know you want to, Gav; I can feel how hard you are."

"If I agree to this, I can't promise I won't hurt you. I'll stop if you want me to, but I may lose my self-control, I might do something you don't like. I don't want you to be afraid to make love to me again."

"Baby, I came here asking you. If I didn't want to, I wouldn't be begging you for it right now."

He stood up with me in his strong arms, my legs wrapped tight around his waist. Pressing me against the wall, he wrapped his fist tightly in my hair, pulling my head back firmly, and then sank his teeth deep into my shoulder.

"The second I saw your beautiful face, I wondered what it would be like to have you tied up, begging for my cock. I wanted to hear you scream while I paddled your perfect ass." He pressed his erection against me. "I still jerk off imagining myself tongue fucking it while I finger your beautiful pussy." His voice was like a growl, "Do you realize devouring your sweet ass is my biggest fantasy? I'm gonna make sure it takes every inch of my rock-hard cock, little girl. Tonight that tight little asshole belongs to me."

"I never knew you were such an ass man; it's all yours, love!"

"I'll tell you what, tonight can be a teaser, an appetizer if you will. If you like it really rough then we can do it one more time, with some toys. It can be the main course. If you don't like it then you need to tell me, and be honest. Your safe word will be 'truth'. Say it and everything will stop, I promise. How does that sound?"

His grin was evil as he stripped off his clothes. As I gazed on his gorgeous body, I answered his question by falling to my knees.

CHAPTER 13

<u>Gavin</u>

I had my beautiful lover begging on her knees, those big, ocean-blue eyes burning with curiosity. She was filled with want, need, for the pleasure she knew awaited her. I'd imagined this day, fantasized about how it would be but never expected it to actually happen. I refused to allow myself to take it too far; we could have some fun, but I wouldn't damage my delicate flower.

"I'm going to ask you one more time, baby girl: are you sure about this?" I pulled her hair, making her face me as I began to jerk off. "Your sweet lover will disappear, and I'll become a dark and dominant man. I'm going to do things to you that you'd never imagine I'd do. I'll fuck any part of you I want, any way I want. It's gonna be rough, and if I lose my self-control I may hurt you, so remember to use your safe word." I bent down for a final, sweet kiss. I was pretty sure she still wanted this.

She softly kissed my lips. "I want this more than anything. I'm all yours, my love."

"Well, then, it's not gonna suck itself so get to work."

Slowly, she began to lick my balls before taking them into her mouth, gently massaging them with her soft tongue. Once she ran her tongue up the full length of my shaft, she fluttered it around the head of my cock as she jerked and teased it. I grabbed her hair tighter and pulled her head forward so I could fuck her gorgeous mouth. She moaned as I made her take my full length down her throat over and over. I looked down and smiled at her each time she gagged. With my fist still wrapped in her hair, I pulled her head back and rubbed her cheek with my dick.

Growling at her, I grabbed her throat. "Is this what you wanted, to be my toy?"

"Yes, please don't stop."

"Stand up and slowly turn around, I want to look at you."

When she stood up, I went to rip off her thong and noticed the ribbon in the back. "Well now, kitten, is that my present?"

"I hope you like them."

"Oh I love them. A perfect ass like yours is my kind of present."

Using my teeth to unwrap my gift, I bit hard into her perfect peach of an ass. "Next time we do this, I'm going to bind your wrists, have you tied while I have my way with you. I can't wait to spank this sexy bottom of yours, my naughty little girl. However, next time you'll be paddled. Just the thought of hearing you cry makes my cock throb. You'll get my belt, too. I'm going to watch your beautiful skin turn pink."

Laying her on the bed, I spread her legs wide and slid my nose through her folds. "Mmm… you smell lovely, my sweet. Are you ready for me?" I slapped her pussy hard. "Answer me!"

"Yes, please. I'm ready."

"Spread your pussy open. Show me the inside." I loved that she kept it waxed, so soft and pink. "What a beautiful sight to see, that pretty little kitty all juicy for me. I want to hear you beg for my cock; tell me how bad you want it." I stuck two fingers inside her and then another. Oh, the beautiful noises she made as I stretched her open.

"Please, I need your dick. Fuck me, own me, make me your whore. I promise I'll be a good girl. I'll take it hard and deep."

"If you want to be a good girl, then you'll take the belt. I'm not waiting for that. I'm going to whip this glorious body so hard you'll feel it for days. This is really going to hurt you, but I'm going to love it. Do you want to be my good girl?"

"Yes, please. Will you let me get it for you?"

"That's my sweet princess!" She got my belt from my pants and fell to her knees in front of me, holding my belt up. "You came here tonight dressed like a naughty girl, begging for my cock. I'm going to whip you into shape, and if you can take it, I'll reward you with the fucking of a lifetime."

Wrapping the belt around my fist for a tighter grip, I had her get on all fours. Each time the leather stung her, she screamed, and each scream made my dick impossibly harder. I gave her four strokes before dropping the belt and quickly rammed my dick into her, making her scream again. Slamming deep into her, I squeezed her throat and growled into her ear.

"This body is mine, and you'll take whatever I give you." Flipping her onto her back, I licked the length her face. "Spread your legs wider and play with that pretty pussy." Watching her play with herself was such a turn-on. "You belong to me now. Don't you dare think otherwise."

My need to be inside her had come full force as I drilled into her, deeper and harder until I could hear my balls slapping her ass. She moaned and bucked as my body devoured hers. I sank my teeth deep into her shoulder again, drawing blood. I can't explain why, but the taste of the mixture of her blood and sweat almost made me cum. It was so raw; I was an animal, and she was my prey.

"Suck my tongue!"

The feeling of her beautiful mouth sucking my tongue in a slow and steady rhythm drove me to the edge. Her body shook, and her pussy clenched, milking the cum from my exploding prick. I massaged her breasts and caressed every inch of her body as she lay in front of me, still coming down from her intense orgasm. Dipping my fingers inside her, I coated them with my juices before stuffing them in her mouth. "Good girl, I love seeing you feed off of me."

I quickly bent her over the bottom of the bed and stood behind her, rubbing the heat from her beautiful ass as I gently kissed every inch. I sank my teeth into her sweet flesh, marking her, claiming what was mine. Each bite caused her to moan louder; she loved it. Finally, I fell to my knees and spread her cheeks.

"The sight of your ass makes my dick rock hard. I can't believe I finally get to taste it." I fluttered my tongue around her tight, puckered hole before slowly pressing a finger in to open it.

"Tonight, you got your fantasy, kitten; now, I'm about to get mine." The gorgeous cheeks of her ass closed in on my face as I lapped at her forbidden area. I plunged my tongue deep inside to get it nice and wet, preparing it for the brutal pounding I was about to give her.

"Are you ready for me, baby? I've been dreaming of this since the day I met you."

Gripping her hips, I gently pressed my cum-covered cock against her hole, slowly guiding my dick inside her inch by inch without hurting her. Once I was inside her, I couldn't control myself, and after a few slow strokes, I had to pick up the pace. I became an animal again, savage and mean. "I'm gonna tear this tight little asshole up. You feel so fucking good." I dug my nails into one of her hips and wrapped my fist in her hair. "Do you like this fat cock in your tight ass?"

She moaned and yelled as I fucked her. "Yes, I love it, oh my God. Fuck me hard."

"You want it hard, here you go."

I pounded every inch of my huge cock deep inside her ass. I could feel her insides stretching around me. I don't think I've ever cum so hard in my life. My hands ran up and down her back, caressing the soft skin as I pulled out of her. Climbing into the bed, what I imagined would be an awkward silence was quite the opposite. Her smile was ear to ear, and she was still breathing deeply with soft moans.

She purred into my ear, "Baby, that was amazing! I've never felt so desired, so needed. My entire body is still tingling. We need round two sooner rather than later. By the way, feel free to fuck my ass whenever you want to. I fucking love it!"

"Oh yeah, I've unleashed the inner freak? No need to beg me for that baby girl; as long as I can eat it a little, I'll gladly ravage that beautiful behind upon request. Now snuggle with me."

CHAPTER 14

Claire

I woke up to Tyler bouncing on top of me, nuzzling in between us to make herself comfortable.

"I dropped the boy off at your mom for some party. She called me and said she wanted to take him. So tell me, was it good that I kept Miles last night?"

I rolled onto my stomach and the sheets moved off me, showing marks from our sexual escapade. "I love you so much. I've never had that much fun in bed."

"Claire, you look like a goddamn chew toy." She looked over at Gavin with anger in her eyes. "What the fuck did you do to her Gavin?"

He sat up getting serious and defensive. "She begged me for it. I told her it wasn't a good idea, but she's my future wife, and she's going to get whatever she asks for, especially in the bedroom."

"You're right, it's not my place to say anything. I will say you two are fucking freaks. I've had rough sex before, but it didn't leave me looking like this!" She gently traced the outline of Gavin's bite-marks on my lower back and butt with her finger, her eyes full of confusion. "I would have never pegged you for the kinky type." She ran her hands over where the belt had been, softly caressing the slight sting that remained. When she noticed the bite mark on my shoulder that had broken skin, she kissed it, as if trying to make it go away.

"Are you sure you're okay?"

"I'm sure, Ty! Believe me, I wanted this. I begged him for it; it was my fantasy, and he knew just what to do to make it real." I put my face next to hers with our lips almost touching. "Haven't you ever wondered what it would be like to become the one thing that can sexually please someone you love in every possible way, to break the barriers of what's considered normal? I was fucked harder and dirtier than I could have imagined, and it felt amazing."

One hand caressed my cheek and she ran her thumb over my lip. It must have seemed odd for Gavin to see us like that; he'd never seen that side of us. There had been quite a bit of petting and touching over the years, as well as a few more intimate moments. I started to breathe a little deeper and my eyes closed. I was visibly aroused by her touch until I saw Gavin's face. I didn't want him mad or hurt. Technically, this was no different from what Cole used to do to me.

Tyler stopped and moved her hand. "I'm sorry, Gav, I shouldn't have touched her like that. Please don't be mad at her." She was practically begging him. "I'm leaving, I'll see you guys later."

He pulled her back in the middle, "Did I tell you to stop? Did I even look upset?"

"But, why aren't you mad at me?"

"All you did was go over bite marks that I put there and touch her face. I'm not blind or stupid; I know there's a twist on your friendship that isn't talked about." He looked at me and raised an eyebrow. "I've already told Claire: it's a show I'd love to watch." He kissed my hand and looked at Tyler. "I've also heard through the grapevine that the two of you were pretty open about your playtime in the past. I was serious when I said she could have whatever she asks me for. Continue ladies!"

I wasn't sure what to think, how to process this. It wasn't something I'd expected. I know Tyler didn't either. Part of me wanted to be pissed at him for not being upset, but the other part of me loved the openness and trust he had.

Tyler broke the awkward silence. "I really should go, as tempting as the offer is, this isn't right. He's your fiancé. I can't."

I couldn't help myself. "You don't need to touch him. We haven't played together in quite a while. If you don't mind him watching, I'll give you exactly what I know you love. Why don't you let me eat your pussy, sweetheart; we both know you'll love it." Gavin's eyes pinched shut, trying to fight the hard-on he was getting. "If not, I won't mention it again. Your choice, lover."

She looked at Gavin and smiled with a slight nod. He pulled the covers off himself baring his amazing body and gifted length, so thick and hard. As his hand wrapped around his dick, Tyler's eyes filled with lust. I pressed my lips to hers, kissing her as we ripped her clothes off. Crawling on top of her, I kissed the tip of her nose. My voice was low. "I see you staring at his cock, but I can't blame you. Trust me, he knows how to work every inch of it. I want to make this a little dirty. Ready to have some fun?"

"Yes, but I want to watch him fuck you. I want to see that dick in motion, and then I'll eat you after he's done. I want to taste him."

With her hips grinding against me, I could sense her desire. I looked at Gavin, silently asking permission to take charge, and he gave me a lustful smile and nod.

"I want you to eat my pussy until I cum all over your

beautiful face. Then, if you're both okay with it, I'll let you have some of that big dick that I know you want."

Her soft tongue swept between the folds of my pussy and deep inside me before she made her way to my clit. She licked and sucked until my whole body began to shake. I hadn't been with her in years; her sweet touch was like a drug to me. I could never stay away for long without needing to come back. Cole had loved it, but he never touched her. Kayleb was dead set against it so it never happened. We were together shortly after the accident, I was curled in bed with her crying, and it just happened, but that was the last time. I couldn't hold myself together any longer. Between the feeling of her soft tongue and the look on Gavin's face as he stroked his beautiful cock, my body erupted in the most magical orgasm. He climbed over and rolled me onto all fours, fucking me hard from behind. Tyler lay there, touching herself as she watched us, rubbing her breasts and pinching her nipples.

"Do you want my cock inside you, Ty? I'll fuck you, but you have to take every inch, and I want to hear you beg."

"Holy shit, yes! I want to feel that huge cock inside me. Please, Gav, show me how good it is."

He pulled her closer to us and started playing with her pussy. "Here I come!"

He slammed into her hard and fast. "I'm gonna stretch this pussy out"

She bucked and screamed into my mouth as I kissed her.

He was going faster now. "Tell me how much you like my big dick!"

She parted her lips to answer him but exploded on him. Watching her cum was such a turn-on. I pushed him away and shoved my face against her pussy. I felt her body shake as her thighs squeezed my head.

"I need some more of you, baby girl. I want some more of your tight little pussy." He turned back into the animal from last night, growling and pulling my hair as he fucked me again. He pulled out, and with a loud moan, he painted my ass cheeks with his cum. "You want a taste of me, Ty? Come get it then."

Grabbing her by the hair, he pushed her face to my ass and made sure she licked every drop off. Making sure she didn't swallow, she pressed her lips to mine, sweeping his thick, salty juices back and forth in our kiss. We collapsed on the bed with me between them.

He looked like a teenager who'd gotten his first peek at porn, "What the fuck did I do to deserve something as hot as that?"

We both laughed at him, and I gave him a peck on the lips. "You're welcome!"

He smacked both our asses at the same time. "Let's get dressed before I'm tempted to ask for round two."

CHAPTER 15

Claire

I was on the way to drop Miles at school and Winston called.

"How's my favorite wedding planner doing?"

"I'm good, except I feel like I traded my dick in for a vagina because this is all making me want to get married one day," Winston groused.

"Don't say that in front of Tyler or there's gonna be a double wedding," I warned.

"There may be a double wedding anyway; Dylan won't shut up about Tara."

"Aww, that's so cool. I hope he gave her some; the girl hasn't had a man in years."

"As far as I've heard, your girl doesn't want it. He said he tried, but she stopped him when he tried to go under the clothes. Dylan's not used to that. Girls literally throw themselves at him. That's why he doesn't do the girlfriend thing; he's usually one and done. He's got Tara programmed in his real phone, and she has her own ring tone. Not many girls even know his actual phone number. No girl has ever been programmed in, and the only ones with their own ringtones are his mom and two sisters. Her ringtone is "Smile" by Uncle Kracker. You may be responsible for introducing him to the only woman who can put a collar on his ass."

"Tara Cross does have a nice ring to it," I mused.

"Well, I think she's clipped his balls already, and he hasn't even gotten to third base. I never thought I'd see the day. Anyway, where are you?"

"Driving Miles to school."

"I'm close; I'm going to meet you there."

I walked out of the school after taking Miles in, and Winston was leaning on my car. He gave me a hug, kissed my cheek, and waved at someone. I turned and saw Sasha giving me a dirty look.

"Friend of yours?"

"Hardly. That's the tramp who tried to steal Gavin from me."

"Yeah, well, I'm not sure even Miss America could do that. You seem to have that dude pretty well wrapped around your finger."

She rolled her eyes at me and flipped me off; she must have heard me call her a tramp. I have to admit it's a rush being friends with Winston and Dylan, especially in front of people like Sasha. I wondered if he knew about the threesome. He and Tyler aren't an official thing, so technically, she didn't do anything wrong, but it might piss him off enough to be done with her.

"I'm taking you to breakfast; put this on." He handed me his helmet, and I hopped onto his bike. It was sweet, a cobalt blue Harley Davidson Fat Boy. I wanted a bike so badly. Maybe one day I'd do more than ride bitch. As liberating as it feels being on the back holding onto a sexy, alpha male type, I want the power. We pulled into Ace's and got ourselves seated.

"So what's the occasion? I figured you were calling to talk about the barbecue place for the wedding."

"No occasion, just two friends enjoying a meal and some coffee. We also have a few things to talk about. Don't worry, nothing bad!"

"These waitresses are getting wet panties staring at you. It's kind of annoying. How do you get used to not being able to eat in peace?"

"I'll let you know once I get there." He paused and turned serious. "Claire, I know about the threesome. Tyler felt like it would be wrong to keep it from me. She didn't want to hide anything just in case this thing we have going on ends up being something." He gave me a reassuring smile. "It's okay; we aren't a couple. I'd be a liar if I said I wasn't extremely jealous that he got you both and I didn't, but that's just my dick talking."

I had to blush a little. "I was hoping you wouldn't push her away because of it. It won't happen again, I promise. I'd like to know how much she told you."

"Everything, that's why I'm jealous. It had to be a real power trip to watch two incredibly gorgeous women make out with a mouthful of your cum; that's some porn star shit. She did love it; that's why she felt the need to tell me. I'm glad she did, it made me think about a lot of things. I've only been hanging out with her for a little over a week now, and I feel like I know her better than any woman I've been with. She's the real deal. She's funny, sweet, beautiful inside and out, and she's honest. Never once have I felt like she wanted to spend time with me because of my job or money."

"She's not that kind of girl. All she ever wanted was to own her own coffee shop. She'd draw layouts and write ideas in the back of her notebooks in high school. She waitressed for years until she had the money to do it. My girl is a self-made, independent woman. She's as real as they come, although she can be a bit stubborn, but it's part of who she is."

"The thing is, she told me over the phone. I didn't know what to say so I told her I'd call her back, and I didn't. I want to ask her to commit to me. I want this to be official. Hopefully, she doesn't think I'm nuts. It just feels right. If she says yes, it's hands off for Gavin." He lifted my chin and looked in my eyes. "Did you catch the *Gavin* part of that statement? Tyler told me how you two are, that she could never give you up permanently. She said it's not something that happens too often, but if it does, she can't say no. It's okay; I'll share her, but only with you. I don't expect us to have threesomes, but if something happens with you two, I want to know about it, that's all I ask."

"Why are you so okay with it?"

"She was honest with me. She told me how much she loves you, and I respect that. I won't be okay with another man touching her, though, or even watching without me there to see it. How about we get out of here and go get me a girlfriend!"

We got my car from the school and went to the Java Spot. When I walked in with Winston, Tyler looked kind of worried. "It's all good, hun. Nothing's changed with us."

She looked at Winston. "Huh?"

"I told Claire I was okay sharing you with her because of your honesty about your relationship. Gavin, as well as anybody else, is hands off, and you tell me if and when you two hook up." He rubbed his thumb down the side of her face. "That is, if you want to be my girl."

"Why? It hasn't even been two weeks yet. Is it because of

what happened with Gavin, like a territorial thing? I told you already, it won't happen again."

"It just feels right. I can't explain it. I look at you and I see someone who sees me, not Vincent Elliot or a wallet. I see a woman who's going to put me in my place when I fuck up and be honest when she does. Tyler, I feel closer to you than I've ever felt to any woman. Sometimes people just know when they've found the one, and that's what this is. You're the one, doll. You're my person."

She wiped the tears that were starting to well in her eyes. "I don't know what to say."

"Well, at the risk of getting shot down a second time, can I call my mom and tell her I finally have someone I want her to meet?" She ran over to him and jumped into his arms.

"Take her out of here. I have this place handled until the next shift."

"Oh, my God, Claire, I love you."

CHAPTER 16

Claire

    I had forgotten how frustrating working at the coffee shop was. I knew what I was doing, but the nonstop flow and uptight customers who came in around this hour were a pain in the ass. Bartending is nonstop, but the drunk customers are fun, and when I work at my shop, it's more of a hobby than a job. It was for my girl though, and she needed it. I shot Gavin a text telling him where I was if he wanted to stop by after he grabbed Miles from school.

    In between customers, I thought about how insane the past few days had been. I'd done things I'd never imagined myself doing, or even wanted to do. Gavin took me to a place I now know that I love. I feel a sexual freedom that I never knew existed. He's my other half, my best friend, my lover, and in a week, he'll be my husband.

    As if things weren't interesting enough already, in walked Sammie, the girl from KC's and the dog park. "Hi again."

    She gave me a dirty look and rolled her eyes, nothing like the other day. "So what? Do you own the whole strip of stores?"

    Not sure if it was sarcasm or just her being a bitch, I let out a little laugh, "No, just helping my best friend out. This is her place, and she had to leave early. I only own the two you know about."

    "Must be nice."

    I felt really uncomfortable, so I switched subjects. "What can

I get for you?"

"Well, I was going to the tattoo shop to talk to you, but I saw you in here. I had an appointment scheduled for my tattoo next Saturday, but I got a voicemail saying I needed to reschedule because the shop will be closed. I'm just going to get it done earlier in the week. Why are you guys closing?"

"I'm getting married. It's the best spur-of-the-moment decision I've ever made."

"That's nice. Who's the lucky guy?"

"His name is Gavin. He's actually my one of my best friends, but you can't fight love. I'm gaining an absolutely adorable son along with him."

"Yeah, well, I'm going to go reschedule." She stormed out in a huff.

Shortly afterward, Gavin and Miles showed up. "Hey, look, it's my boys!"

"Hey, doll face, I was going to take us all to dinner. How long are you here for?"

"Two people are coming in at 5, and one is a key holder; as soon as she gets here, I'm out! Where do you want to go?"

He kissed my forehead and sat on one of the stools at the bakery bar. "That's up to you. Think about it. How has your day been?"

"It started great. I had breakfast with Winston. He wanted to talk about what happened the other day. Ty told him she liked it so much that she felt guilty. He just wanted to tell me he wasn't mad at her or anything. He said he was jealous of you though, and watching 'the kiss' must have been a big power trip."

"He's not trying to get you, is he? I'm the only one who touches my baby girl, with the exception of Ty every once in a while."

"No, he's not. He specifically said he didn't want me to think he wanted threesomes, but he's willing to share Ty on occasion as long as he's told about it."

"Fair enough, it looks like we're all on the same page. Anything else interesting happen?"

"This wacky chick came in asking why she had to reschedule her tattoo. I saw her in the shop when she was booking the appointment, and she was grilling me hard. I ran into her again while I was walking Calvin, and she was kinda nice in a fake sort of way, but today she was a nasty bitch."

"Multiple personalities sound almost as fun as the spoiled little prep school brats. I did catch this couple arguing in the hallway; they're juniors. The poor kid was pissed because the girl was talking to the rest of the cheerleaders about how hot Mr. Price was. Apparently, the cheerleaders are hot for teacher."

"I'll come to that high school and whup some teenage ass!"

"Well, considering I'm not a dirtbag, you have nothing to worry about."

"Do you have any idea how much I love you?"

"I think I have a pretty good idea, but I love you more! Can I leave Miles here while I go shower and change?"

"Of course. I might put him to work. We'll meet you at home when I'm out of here."

He kissed me goodbye and left. Miles played with my iPad until it was time to go. I wanted to stop and check on things at the shop before we left, so we headed next door. When I walked in, Beth was doing a tattoo, and Tara sterilizing her stuff. I introduced Miles to the new kid I had working at the comic shop. He was a senior in high school and had come in asking for an after school job. The kid knew his stuff, so I hired him on the spot.

"Miles this is Luke; he works for Mommy now."

Luke shook his hand. "It's nice to meet you little man. Hope I see ya around here a bunch. I'll teach you all you need to know about the world of comics."

"Mr. Monster is in the house!" Beth smiled and blew him a kiss. "Hey, boss lady!"

He saw Tara and jumped up onto her. She's his favorite, and he's told Gavin he wants to marry her. "Hey, buddy!" She gave him a big kiss then looked at me. "This boy may have some competition thanks to you, Claire. Dylan is awesome; thanks for the intro."

"I'm glad you two clicked "

"Well, so far so good. He's a total sweetheart, fun and kind of quirky. And let's not forget totally gorgeous."

"I wanted to ask you about a customer. She came in to reschedule her tattoo today; her name is Sammie."

Beth stopped and gave her customer a break. "She's got an infinity symbol on her back. She's getting it thicker with her son's name on it. His name is Miles, too.

"She's a bit of a weirdo, at least toward me, so I don't want to be here when she's getting it done.

Tara checked the books. "Four o'clock Tuesday."

"Good to know. I'm headed home now. Just wanted to check in. Oh, Tara, only a few more days until the show!"

"I hope you don't mind, but I want to bring Dylan."

"Why would I mind? Gavin's coming, and I put Tyler and Winston on the list. I'm off to meet my honey now. He's taking me and the munchkin out for dinner."

I walked into the house and there was a path of rose petals leading to the back porch. The note on the sliding glass door said to send Miles down to the den for pizza with Tyler and Winston. The round table on the porch had place settings and lit candles with more scattered rose petals. I couldn't help smiling ear to ear as I stepped onto the porch. I didn't see Gavin, so I turned to go back in the house to find him, but he was in the doorway, holding a bouquet of tiger lilies. Tears of happiness rolled down my cheeks; I couldn't believe he was doing all this just because.

"Tears? I hope they're happy tears. I know that tiger lilies are your favorite. The roses were for romantic effect, although, I loose points for the candlelight dinner being pizza; I was pressed for time!"

"This is so perfect. Pizza by candlelight sounds wonderful."

"It's safe to say you've turned me into a hopeless romantic, baby girl." He stepped forward and kissed my forehead. "Sweeter than a thousand, my beautiful future wife!"

CHAPTER 17

Gavin

I walked to the side table and turned on the music. I know my lady loves her 90s alternative music and "Luna" by the Smashing Pumpkins is her favorite love song; it really is amazing. I just knew she'd love this.

I held my hand out to her. "May I have this dance?"

She melted against my chest as we danced, and she softly sang the sweet words. Looking in my eyes, she smiled. "This is our moon song."

"I love listening to you sing, sweetheart." I held her tight and kissed her.

As we sat at the table and ate, all I could do was gaze at her beauty. I thought about all the horrible things I'd done in my past that I wasn't proud of, a life most would call repulsive. I was a sexual sadist so to speak. Causing pain used to be the only thing that could get me off. Everything was consensual, but it didn't make it less vile. To be quite honest, I never understood why a woman would want to allow a man to do such nasty things to her.

Having a child changed it all for me. I walked away from that life immediately without question. The second I looked in my son's eyes, I knew there was a God. Miles was a smaller version of me in every way, and when I saw him, I saw a second chance at becoming the man I wanted to be. Then Claire came along, and I learned what home really was. Even before she was mine, I knew she'd be mine. I have been with her at some point every day for the last two years without so much as a kiss, and I waited because I knew she was the one. I hadn't gone more than a month at most without fucking someone since the age of sixteen, but I never once felt the need to even look at another female since the first day I met Claire. She was my center, my best friend, and the only woman I've ever truly loved.

"God made you for me." I didn't mean to say it out loud.

She looked up at me and smiled. Jesus, she was beautiful. I knew I needed to be honest with her about who I was, what I had done before her. It was only fair that she find out before we were married, in case she wanted to walk away.

"Claire, I need to tell you something. I need you to know about my past, about who I was before Miles was born. You need to know everything before you marry me, just in case it makes you change your mind. You may see me as a different person."

"Gavin, I'm not going anywhere. Short of being a child molester or rapist, there's nothing that's gonna change the way I feel about you. Nothing you say can possibly make me stop loving you. Everyone has demons in their past; it's just that some are bigger and badder than others. The man you think will scare me away is long gone. I'm madly in love with the Gavin Price that is sitting across from me. I'll listen to what you have to say, but unless you end us, you're stuck with me forever."

Her warmth and tenderness calmed my nerves. "Well, here it is. I was what some would call a hard-core sexual sadist. I never did anything by force; it was all consensual. It was complete pleasure to watch women in pain, especially when I was causing it. It wasn't like your books; those are different than the shit I've done. There were no contracts, no Dom/sub relationship, no love of any kind. I was part of an underground sex club. I very rarely fucked the same woman twice and didn't know most of their names.

"I became friends with my ex. We'd hung out outside the club a few times, but it was just fucking. She liked to be cut; I liked to cut, so it worked. I never dated any of them. Any woman who was willing to let a total stranger smile and laugh as he burned her pussy with hot wax before fucking her senseless was far from girlfriend material. I've done some things to women that I refuse to let come out of my mouth. Love wasn't in my vocabulary; nobody made me want anything close to a meaningful relationship. It was raw, dirty, and down right dangerous."

Her face was white as a ghost. "You married her; surely you loved her."

"No, I didn't. I didn't have an emotional connection of any kind with her. I told you before we weren't a couple; I only married her because of Miles. One night, the condom broke while we were fucking; I figured she'd get the plan B pill. She was with a lot of men so I didn't even believe Miles was mine until I laid eyes on him. I was hoping I'd form a bond with her, grow to love her over time, but I just couldn't. She's a fuckin' nut job. She must have been on the same page because she filed for divorce and left. I was happy about the divorce, but it sickens me that she left Miles. She signed over all legal rights to him; the only tie they'll ever have is genetic. She wrote in the note that she never wanted to be a mom, said he was my problem to deal with. What woman says that about their child? I'm glad she did though, because now he has you. You are my second chance at life, Claire; I just needed you to know who I use to be."

"Is that why you tried to talk me out of the other night?"

"Yeah, I love you, and the last thing that would ever give me pleasure is to see you in pain. I'd die for you, Claire. I will say the other night was amazing, just enough rough stuff to keep it interesting. I've never bit anyone the way I do you. It's not to hurt you; it's more intimate than anything. I feel like I'm claiming you. It sounds juvenile, but I can't help it. In the heat of the moment, I just feel the need to do it. The fact that you let me spank you is icing on the cake; the idea of seeing my handprint on that perfect ass is fuckin' hot. That has to be it though. I can't go any further with you. I know you're curious, but I can't take you to a darker place because I'm afraid that if I go back there, I won't want to leave. No more domination, no more degradation. You're my queen, not my whore. You will never take my belt again, either. I had fun doing it, but seeing your beautiful body all bruised afterward broke my heart; please don't ask me to do that again. I'll spank you with my hand, but that's where it ends. Is that okay?"

"Listen, I had the greatest sexual experience of my life that night, other than you putting on my engagement ring while making love to me. If you're feeling guilty because you think you hurt me, please don't. It did hurt, but only for a second, then it brought out a side of me that I never knew existed. I loved every second of every part of what we did. Do you feel like what we did was wrong?"

"I don't know. Like I said, I loved doing it, I got lost in a cloud of lust and desire; I took it too far. I just want to be normal."

"Gavin Price, what exactly is classified as normal? Is normal holding in your sexual desires, pretending they aren't there in your mind? How about fucking the woman you love and being forced to hold back, to be someone you're not, is that normal? How long until you end up so miserable from hiding what you want that you don't even want to have sex anymore?"

"Claire, I just—"

"Don't butt in; I'm not done." I grabbed his hand and looked him in the eyes. "Let me tell you what normal is, Gavin. Normal is admitting what you feel and accepting what it is that makes you tic. You enjoy inflicting pain during sex, not in your daily routine. You aren't a woman beater or a rapist. You like extremely rough sex; there's not a damn thing wrong with that." I hated seeing him so torn up inside. "Baby, you were lucky enough to fall for a girl who enjoys receiving what you need to give in order to be fully satisfied. I'm new to all this, but there's no doubt in my mind that I'm going to want to do that again. You said we were made for one another, well this is proof. Biting, spanking, hair pulling, and some dirty talk, if that's part of our sex life then I'm a happy woman, but don't be afraid to do more to me because I fucking loved it. Our bond is unbreakable, Gav, and nobody has ever made me feel the way you do. Give me the pain that will take me to the same place in my mind I was that night, and by doing that, you'll bring yourself back to life."

"No love, you just brought me back to life. I want to…" My words disappeared and my mind clouded. She'd dropped to her knees and unzipped my pants.

"No more talking, I want my dessert! Just close your eyes, my love; I'm going to take my time. This is all about you. I'm gonna make you cum so hard you'll never question my desire for you again."

Moments ago, I was thinking that I was going to lose her and my past would scare her away, but now she is on her knees giving me the most amazing blow job I've ever gotten. I didn't even care that the neighbors might see. I leaned my head back and looked at the stars while the love of my life made love to me with her beautiful mouth.

CHAPTER 18

Claire

    I woke up Sunday morning to a little nuzzle on my chest. Luckily, I'd put on a tank top and panties when I got up in the middle of the night because Miles had climbed into bed and made a pillow out of me. I rubbed his hair as he cuddled against me. "Good morning, love bug!"

    "Good morning, Mommy!" He kissed my belly. "I wanted a little brother, but I'm going to have a little sister first."

    "Miles, there's no baby in there yet."

    "Yes there is. I dreamed it three times, and they were all the same. The pretty angel girl told me that I was going to be a big brother soon, and I needed to protect my baby sister, because that's what big brothers do. She said my baby sister was inside your belly. She was very pretty, she had blonde hair and smiled just like you."

    "Well, Daddy and I would love that. Hopefully, it's true."

    The bedroom door opened and Gavin and Calvin came in. I gave my dog some love. He was still adjusting to living here, but he had Miles to follow around and play with so he was happy. Gavin blew me a kiss. "Miles, I made your breakfast. It's down on the coffee table. Go ahead down and eat; I put on Disney for you."

    "Okay Daddy! Come on, Calvin. Daddy wants to kiss Mommy."

I couldn't help but laugh. "Oh, my God, he's your boy!"

"Well, he's right; I do plan on kissing you. Did you know that breakfast is the most important meal of the day?" He shut and locked the bedroom door before crawling on top of me.

"Well, then, we better not skip it!" I ran my fingers through his gorgeous blond hair and gave him a heated, passionate kiss before nipping at his cheek. "What are you making me for breakfast?"

He had his lustful 'fuck me' face on. He flipped me onto my stomach and tore my panties off. I felt his teeth sink into my bottom on each side followed a hard smack. He massaged the cheeks of my ass and then I felt it, his soft tongue slowly preparing my body for what was next. He pulled on my hair to tilt my head back and put his lips to my ear. In a deep voice, he said, "Baby girl, I'll make you whatever you want after I ravage this beautiful behind."

"Have at it, big boy!" I gave him exactly what I know he loves.

We cuddled in bed for a few minutes but Miles was awake and alone downstairs. I stood up, and Gavin pulled me back down. "Thank you for breakfast, my dear. It was delicious."

"My pleasure, love."

We went downstairs for some couch cuddles and cartoons with Miles. I loved the family time before the craziness of the day.

I kept thinking about what Miles had said. Some people say little kids can see angels, talk to spirits. It was silly, but I wondered if he'd seen Audrey. Had she told him about a little sister? Did she help pick her little soul out? It was a comforting feeling that I wanted so badly to be true. It was too soon to tell, but I hoped we had a pretty princess growing inside me. I was pulled out of my trance when Tara called.

"Hey girlie, what's up?"

"I'm calling to figure out the plan for tonight."

"It starts at 7 o'clock but we need to be there at 6 o'clock. I think I'm just gonna have a late lunch. I'll be too nervous to eat dinner. Want to grab something with me at the diner around 2?"

"Sounds like a plan. What are you wearing?"

"I'm gonna dress up, more of a punk style though. I want to match the type of pictures I'm bringing."

"Good to know. I'll do the same thing. I'm out with Dylan so I gotta go, but I'll see you at 2."

"Later!"

"I'm going to hop in the shower. I'll see you gentlemen in a little bit. Oh, Miles, tell Daddy about your dreams."

"I'll be up in a few to take a shower, too."

I got in and let the hot water relax my muscles. As much as I tried, I couldn't stop wondering, hoping, even wishing Miles' prediction was true. I rubbed my belly and started talking out loud. "Are you in there little one? Did you meet your big sister? Did she help pick you out for us? Jesus, I sound crazy."

"No, you don't, sweetheart." Gavin was standing in the doorway with tears in his eyes. "Don't you for one second think that Audrey won't know the baby we'll have. Be it now or later, we'll be pregnant, and she will have been a part of it. She's your guardian angel, sweetheart, our guardian angel, and she's always with us."

My tears fell uncontrollably, so he stepped into the shower fully clothed and hugged me as I cried. "I never got to say goodbye. I just want to hold her one more time. Out of everything that happened, she's the one thing I can't get over." I was trying to catch my breath. "I just want my little girl back, Gavin. I want Audrey." We slid to the floor of the shower, and he cradled me, holding me tight until I ran out of tears.

He wrapped me in my bathrobe, picked me up, and carried me to the bedroom. He stripped off his wet clothes and climbed into bed with me. Pulling me next to him so we were face to face, he kissed my forehead. "You won't ever get over it. She's your daughter. All you can do is be strong and live with it, and you do a damn good job at that. Every once in a while you're entitled to a breakdown, and I'm always going to be here for you when it happens. I'm your safe place, Claire. Now close your eyes for a little bit, and I'll wake you up in time to get ready."

At 12:30, Gavin gently ran his fingers up and down my cheek to wake me up. I opened my eyes and smiled. "Thank you for taking care of me. I haven't had a breakdown like that in months."

"I'll always take care of you, baby girl!"

"I should get up and going so I can meet Tara." I kissed his fingers one by one. "Do you know what might make my day get better?" I pulled him so he was sitting on the bed next to where I was lying.

"Why don't you tell me, and just maybe I can help you out."

I pulled him in for a kiss. "Will you eat my pussy, love? I want to cum all over that sexy face."

"Trust me, that's a request I'll never deny; I fucking love the way you taste. Lie down and relax, beautiful, I got this."

CHAPTER 19

Claire

I pulled into Ace's Diner a little after 2 o'clock and saw Tara's car there. I went in to meet her and was surprised to see her without Dylan. "Hey, sweetness, where's your other half?"

"I let him go play with Winston for a while. Between Tyler and me, their bromance has been struggling. I owe you big time for the intro!"

"So did you hop on the magic stick? Inquiring minds want to know."

"Really Claire, the 'magic stick'? What is he? 50 Cent?" She was laughing. "I haven't heard that song in forever! The answer is no, I haven't. He's tried a few times to get really hot and heavy, but I just can't. I really like being around him, and he's beyond sexy, but realistically speaking, I've only known the guy for two weeks. It's crazy that I have a Pinterest file titled *YUMMY* and ninety percent of the pictures are of him, yet I can't bring myself to do more than kiss him. Explain that to me."

The waiter came to take our order. He'd heard us talking because he looked Tara up and down and smiled. "My stick is very magical, so if it doesn't work out with Mr. Yummy then let me know."

"I'm flattered, but the man has me hooked!"

"He's a lucky man; you're like a decorated version of Snow

White. Flawless beauty with just enough punk rock to make a skater boy swoon."

"Wow, you know how to make a girl blush. I just might send my little sister in here. We have different dads. Hers is Native American so she's a decorated Pocahontas."

We both ordered french toast with bacon and as we sat and ate we continued our talk about her and Dylan.

"So how serious is this? Are we talking fun with a friend or meet the parents?"

"I'm not sure really. I know I'm really into him, and I think he's on the same page, I hope so anyway." She made a worried face and sipped her coffee. "What if I'm just a way to kill time? I've heard he can be quite the ladies' man and never has a girlfriend. How can I tell? What happens when some beauty queen spreads her legs? I just can't be that girl, you know, the one who fucks him just because he's Dylan Cross. That might just be what ends whatever this is."

"It's not really my place to say it, but since you're so upset, I'm going to as long as it doesn't leave this table. I know for a fact he's way into you. Winston told me you've clipped his balls. You're the only girl he's ever programed into his phone, and you have your own ringtone. He also said the only people with special ringtones are Dylan's mom and sisters. Yours is "Smile" by Uncle Kracker. Stop stressing, honey; this is something real, and it will happen in your own time." I squeezed her hand for reassurance. "I need to thank Detective Dickhead for being a perv. If he hadn't fondled me in Starbucks, I wouldn't have met them."

"We can send him a pair of your panties!"

I couldn't help but laugh. "I'm sure Gavin would love that! Actually, he probably would if they were post ejaculation panties;

he's big on marking his territory. What better way to piss off the man who's obsessed with your girl than to send him her thong soaked in your semen?"

"That's pretty gangstah! It's pretty fucking gross, too."

"I settled on two different pictures of you, the one where you're spread eagled and the Frankenstein tattoo one. I'm using the 50s style zombie picture we took here last year, the *Thriller* dance from the party, the picture of Gavin and Tyler dressed in Freddy and Jason costumes fighting each other, and the one of Miles dressed as the kid from *Pet Cemetery*."

"I love that one. That kid is too much. I remember he carried Beth's poor cat around the whole day. That cat really does look like the one from the movie. It's creepy."

"I made a bunch of prints and business cards for KC's also. Oh, I forgot to mention the owner wants to keep one of you to hang in the gallery."

"Shut up!"

"For real. This all seems too good to be true. I have everything I could wish for. It's about time life dealt me a good hand!" I debated whether to tell her what happened earlier, but decided against it. "Did you hear Ty and Winston are official? It's so soon, but I guess sometimes you just know you've found the one."

"I heard about it, and I have to say I'm a little envious that I'm not there with Dylan, but I'm totally happy for them. I'll settle for the fact that I've been with him every day since we met, and he calls me beautiful more than he uses my name. Pet names are fun to have." She raised an eyebrow at me. "So what's this I hear about a certain threesome that took place?"

"Wow, who told you?"

"I'll never tell!"

"It just happened. Gavin and I had some hard-core fuckage the night before that left a lot of bite marks on me. Ty saw them the next morning when she came into my room and bugged out on him. She started touching and kissing them and then got up to leave. He pulled her back down, and before I knew it, there was a lot of touching, sucking, and fucking followed by a sexy cum-shared kiss. It's the craziest thing I've ever done, but I loved every second of it."

"Sounds pretty hot! I've seen you two kissing before, but that kiss would have been fun to watch!"

"I didn't know you were into girls."

"It's been a long time, but I've had my share of pretty ladies. I had a steady girlfriend in college for about a year, and then I was a dick and fucked her brother. Let's just say that didn't end well. The shitty thing is she was way more fun in bed."

"Holy shit! I never would have pegged you for the asshole in a break-up. My sweet little Tara is a cheater."

"Shut it, woman! Let's get out of here. Lunch is on me."

We left the diner, and when I got to my car, I saw the words "HE'S MINE" keyed into the side of my car and all four of my tires slashed. My hands started shaking; I'm not sure if it was anger or fear.

"Tara, wait!" I knew I had screamed for her but couldn't hear my own words because of the thumping in my head.

"Jesus Christ, who the fuck did this? You call Gavin, and I'll call the cops."

Gavin got there before the cops did. "Holy shit! Who the

hell—"

I cut him off. "*You* tell *me*. You know you're the only man in my life, so who else would this crazy ass bitch be referring to? Just tell me the fucking truth, Gavin. Who were you fucking before we were official? I know there's nobody else now, but who did you cut off last week? It's got to be the same chick who left that picture under my door." I was screaming so loud they must have heard me across town.

"I told you before, I haven't touched another girl since the day I met you. That's the truth, and you better fucking believe me." He ran his fingers through his hair in frustration. He looked like he was going to cry. "Because if you don't believe me, then we don't have the bond I thought we did. I never once lied to you, and I never will."

Tears poured down my cheeks. "I'm sorry, Gavin. I believe you. I'm just scared and angry. I'm so mixed up."

"It's okay, honey. We gotta figure out who's gone all stalker before someone gets hurt."

The cops pulled up in in a black SUV, and I wondered why it wasn't just a patrol car. The doors opened, and of course, Cole and Morgan got out of the car.

Gavin threw his hands in the air. "Wonderful, just fucking fantastic. Of all the cops in Acceta, we get you two LA dickheads."

Cole came up and hugged me. "Are you all right? I was at the Acceta station when the call came in. I told them you were family, and they let us take it."

Gavin looked furious. "She'll be just fine if you keep your hands off of her. You can do your job without touching my fiancée!"

"I'm okay, Cole. I just want to figure this out before anything really bad happens. A picture of Gavin and me was pushed under the door to the shop the other day. I didn't take it seriously, but now, I wish I had."

Cole turned to Gavin with a serious look on his face. "I want you to put aside your hatred for me and look at it like this: we both love her and would do anything to protect her. I lost her because I allowed myself to become a piece of shit woman beater who'd fuck any whore who'd spread her legs. I was too dumb and drunk to realize all I needed was the goddess I married. I let alcohol ruin my life, and by the time I changed my ways, I was too late, she loves you. I'll never get a second chance. You won, so stop dick measuring."

Morgan just stood there for a minute then looked at Gavin. "If I don't help you, Grammy will disown me."

Cole focused on Gavin. "Is there anyone who comes to mind that could have done this? Any ex-girlfriends or women you rejected? Were you sleeping with anyone else?"

"No. I have an ex-wife who is somewhere in NYC, but she left me five years ago. I've been trying like hell to get Claire for the last two years, so there's nobody. There's that Sasha girl though, but I doubt she'd do this. She's just a chick who tried to get me to sleep with her, but I shot her down."

"I'm going to want to speak to her anyway."

I chimed in on their conversation. "She's an immature young girl, but she's also a single mom. She's not going to get in trouble with the law because she got shot down for a booty call. I really need to get going though. I have to get ready for the expo. Can we finish all this tomorrow?"

"Yeah, I'll call you tomorrow. Leave me your car keys. I'll text you the info on when and where you can get pick it up." He kissed his thumb and pressed it to my cheek. "I'm going to figure this out. I promise I will." He looked at Gavin. "You won, be good to our girl."

CHAPTER 20

Claire

I was determined tonight would be amazing and to let go of the dark cloud over my head. I had my prints and canvases put together with the business cards. All that was left was to get myself ready. I hopped into the shower and thought about what to wear, dressy but punk, hot and kind of badass.

The bathroom door opened. "The sitter just picked up Miles. I want to talk about today. I need to know that you believe me when I say there's nobody else."

"All I have to say is I believe you, and you need to believe me when I say that. I don't want to talk about any of this tonight, though." I stepped out of the shower and pressed my wet body against him. I ran my fingers through his soft hair as he held me close, his strong hands running up and down my wet back. "I'm blocking out the negativity of today and focusing on the positive, and so far, every positive had something to do with you."

He gave me his Prince Charming smile and ran his hands from my belly up to my breasts, cupping them in his palms. Gently, he stroked his thumbs over my nipples as he stared into my eyes, like he was searching my soul. He fell to his knees in front of me and put his lips on my belly. "I love you more than life, Claire. I don't know why Miles said what he did today, but I hope it's true. You own every piece of me; you have since the day we met. Now that I finally have you, I want nothing more than to put a tiny little life inside you. I want to make you a mother again."

I pulled him up and kissed his hands. "You already have. You gave me a son I adore, and if you haven't put a little peanut inside me yet, then you will soon enough."

"You should go get dressed. If you stay naked in front of me too much longer, I'm gonna bend you over this sink."

"You're an ass, but I still love you"

He gave me a hard slap on the ass as I left the bathroom. I looked through my clothes and found nothing that worked. I was starting to get nervous. I wanted to look just right for the occasion. I remembered Tara had left a bag with a few outfits she didn't wear for me to try on, and there it was. My punk rock princess had saved the day. The maroon skirt had black skulls on it and ended mid-thigh. It looked great with the short-sleeve, open-back, mock turtleneck that showed all my upper body tattoos. For an extra twist of punk, I put on my maroon and pink Iron Fist zombie heels with my black, thigh-high stockings. With my long hair flowing, my fingers and toes painted black, and just a little makeup, I was ready to go. I looked in the mirror and actually felt sexy.

I headed downstairs, hoping Gavin would like my outfit as much as I did. He was sitting on the couch watching an old episode of *Hard Law* when he saw me. My irresistible lover looked so fine dressed in his dark jeans and a tight, black, dress shirt, which enhanced his muscles. I couldn't wait to run my hands up and down his rock-hard abs. When he had his hair tied back the way he did, his handsome face and bright blue eyes lit up the room.

"Well, what do you think?" I slowly spun around for him to get a full view. I strolled toward the front of the TV, but he was already walking toward me, undoing his belt. He lifted my skirt and quickly bent me over the love seat.

"Well now, I see someone wants to be my naughty girl. You

know what I like to do to naughty girls, don't you?" With a hard smack to my ass, he shoved the crotch of my panties to the side and started rubbing my swollen clit, changing paces back and forth from slow to fast. "You're so fuckin' hot. Just looking at you makes me hard." He gripped my throat and his dominant voice growled in my ear. "I'm gonna take what's mine now, kitten. I'm gonna fuck you 'til you scream." Shoving himself deep inside me, he pounded hard and fast while tightly wrapping his fist in my hair. The harder he pulled on it, the harder he fucked me. My knees went weak, and I felt my orgasm building up, my inner thighs soaked with my arousal. My pussy was throbbing, and I could feel it clenching. "That's it, darlin', squeeze my cock with that tight little pussy." We erupted, cumming hard together. "Tell me, love, whose pussy is this?"

"Oh, it's all yours!"

"Good girl." He bit my neck then pulled himself out of me.

"I guess you like the outfit." I smiled then adjusted myself. "I need to go clean myself up really quick since you can't keep your hands off me."

"You, my dear, are intoxicating. Don't clean up too much. I want you to walk around with my cum soaking your panties. I want you nice and juicy, and it drives me wild when you smell like me."

"I love when you're so primal, baby. It turns me on to know how badly you want me." I tugged his beard a little. "Let's go before I saddle you for round two, I don't want to be too late."

We met Tara and Dylan at the Penne Vista and were greeted by Sarah Jenkins. She shook our hands then proceeded to hug Gavin, pressing her breasts against him. When she finally let go of him, she ran her hands down his chest. "Nice to see you, Mr. Price! Can I call you Gavin?"

"Of course you can." I could see how awkward he was feeling, but he held it together.

Tara whispered in my ear. "She'd like to call him more than that while he plows her out."

"You're an asshole, Tara!" I had to force myself not to laugh.

Sarah turned to us and smiled. "Right this way, ladies."

As we were escorted to our spot, Gavin and Dylan took seats at the bar. It was the most interesting bar I'd ever seen. It had a sapphire blue top, and the entire bottom was a huge fish tank full of exotic fish. They had to be saltwater fish because they looked like they were straight out of *Finding Nemo*. I had to take a picture to show Dave; he'd love it.

This gallery was huge. Only a wing of it was being used tonight, and that on its own was impressive. The bright white walls and pillars were a perfect contrast to the black marble floors. Black leather love seats were randomly placed next to glass end tables. There were sapphire blue suede benches wrapped around the bottom of each pillar. Once I started hanging my pictures, I noticed Sarah's facial expression had changed a bit. She was looking at my hand with what I wanted to think was an unintentional grimace on her face. Tara smiled at her, which seemed to snap her back into focus.

"What a beautiful ring. Who's the lucky man?" She glanced over at the guys. "I'm assuming that gentleman over there with Gavin."

Tara chimed in before I could answer. "No, that one is mine. Gavin finally picked up his balls and told Claire how he felt. Can you believe he bought that rock two months ago? They weren't even a couple. He thought of her when he saw it and knew one day he'd get the nerve to propose." She looked at Gavin then back to me. "When you're as tight as these two are, dating isn't necessary."

I smiled at Tara. "Enough about me!"

"Own your story, girl. It's not often people get a real life happily ever after." She had a point, so I let her finish. "For the last two years they've been joined at the hip, they're best friends. No physical relationship at all, just the pure love of two soul mates waiting for the right moment to admit to themselves and each other that they were meant to be." She took a sip of her wine and smiled. "Now someone needs to write a love story about that!"

"Well, Ms. Michaels, you're one lucky woman."

"Yes I am!" I smiled and waved at Gavin, blowing him a kiss as I watched her walk away. "Way to be a bitch, Tara, and good job staking your claim on Dylan. I'm kind of thinking she'd rather have Gavin though."

"Do ya think?" She laughed until she noticed a blonde Barbie-type walk up to Dylan. He was smiling as they were talking, and he jotted something down on a piece of paper. She shoved it in her little Michael Kors clutch bag and continued to flirt with him.

"Claire, what do I do? He just gave her his number, and I can't go say anything; it's not my place." Her face turned white as a ghost and she got shaky. "Oh God, I'm going to be sick. I should have just fucked him, what was I thinking?" Why did I even think I had a real chance? Just look at her. She's the total opposite of me. She's the type I see him wanting to be with. Girls like me don't walk the red carpet. I don't want all that. I just want him."

"Tara, chill for a minute. Regardless of the fact that you aren't interested in him for his career, the public looks at him as Aaron Dean. Women are going to approach him, and he's going to have to be personable, make small talk, sign an autograph, and maybe take a picture. She approached him. He chooses to spend all his time with you. Shit Tara, he's here because of you." I hugged her so she'd calm down.

We looked at them, and Dylan was pointing at Tara. He winked at her and called her over. Barbie looked at us and walked away. There was a half-hour left until the doors opened so we headed to the bar to be with them. Gavin pulled me in for a hug and kissed my forehead.

"Sweeter than a thousand!" Flashing his sweet smile, he kissed my hand and whispered in my ear. "I hope you didn't mind Mr. Dominant sneaking out before we left. No matter how hard I try, sometimes I can't control myself with you."

"I like when he decides to visit. There's nothing like a good spanking every now and again."

"I hope you know all that dirty talk is just playful. I don't ever want you to think I consider you my property; you're my queen. If anything, you run the show, you have me under your spell."

I ran my hands up and down his firm chest. "I know, baby."

Dylan pulled Tara next to him and lifted her chin. "I hope you don't mind, but I told that chick who was just undressing me with her eyes that I was here with you." He softly kissed her lips. "Tara, I saw your face when she came up to me. I only signed an autograph. I wouldn't take a picture with her, and I damn sure didn't give her my number. Am I here with my beautiful date, who I can't seem to tear myself away from, or my friend who happens to be a girl? I'm pretty sure it's a date; at least, I was hoping that's what it was. Women will flirt with me, and I'll smile and talk to them because I have to." The tip of his tongue ran up her neck before giving her little nibbles. "I'm here with you, gorgeous. No random fangirl is changing that."

"I'm not even gonna lie, I was a little intimidated by her, but you called me gorgeous. Mr. Cross, you've just made me a very happy girl."

Tyler snuck up behind us and pinched my ass. "Tonight is the night, doll. I'm so proud of you!"

Dylan nodded to Winston. "Fangirls are among us." He picked up Tara and spun her around. "This one needs some thicker skin if she's gonna be with me." He gave her a peck on the cheek. "It's almost 7. You guys should go stand by your pictures."

Tara and I made our way back as the doors opened. Waiters in tuxedos floated through the crowd with champagne and hors d'oeuvres. Some people seemed like true horror fans, some we could tell were going to re-sell. My pictures of Tara were big sellers, and the diner one was a hit, also. The picture of Miles was just for display; I didn't feel right selling a picture of my son.

Tyler took over my station so Gavin and I could look around for a bit. We looked at the different types of pictures people had. There were so many different takes on horror. I fell in love with a picture of a crow perched on a black metal fence; it reminded me of the movie. I talked to the photographer a little and ended up buying the canvas for the shop. Gavin pointed out a picture that made the ones I took of Tara look like they were from a children's book. It looked like a horrible picture of a rape.

"That's too raw even for me, and I can be a sick fuck." He shook his head at the photographer. "Not to mention that kind of looks like my ex."

"I think she looks really familiar too. She kinda looks like that chick from the shop who creeps me out. I can't picture her doing that though, but who knows."

We walked up to the picture and stared at it for a minute before approaching the photographer. I began to talk to a guest who'd recognized me from KC's while Gavin spoke to him.

"Who is this in the picture?"

He shrugged his shoulders. "Not sure what her name is. She's a freak and a half, and a loony bitch, but she's hot as hell and was literally begging them to do that to her. She signed off on me taking pictures, but I can't remember her name." He looked at me and then at Gavin, "Your girl is beautiful and looks like a real lady. Why would you look twice at this tramp?"

"She looks just like my ex. Her name is Mara. She has different hair and more tattoos than I remember, but I haven't seen her in five years."

"I took this about two weeks ago at a party in LA. Sam, that's it, her name is Sam."

Gavin said goodbye to the photographer and stepped back toward me. "Let's go see how Ty's doing."

"Tara just went into the bathroom. I'm going to do my girlfriendly duty and join her. I'll meet you back there."

I went in the bathroom and Barbies 1 and 2 were in powder room section loading more makeup on their faces. They were talking about Tara, and I knew she would hear them.

"Can you believe he's here with that freak show? It has to be a contest or publicity thing. There is no way someone like him would choose that over this." She ran her hand down her body.

Barbie 2 chimed in, "Maybe she's a co-worker. Either way,

he's leaving here with us. Threesome tonight, girl!"

There was no way I could keep my mouth shut. I was hoping once she heard my voice, Tara would come stand up for herself. I joined them in front of the mirror, acting like I wanted to touch up my lipstick. "Oh, I recognize you. You're the girl who tried to pick up Dylan. Sorry, but he prefers to spend his time with a classy woman."

She gave a fake laugh. "If you call rainbow hair and a face full of metal classy, then you're deranged."

"Wow, big words for a Barbie doll. She has more class than both of you combined."

Tara approached us. "Class and self-respect. Honey, he hasn't left my side for weeks, and I still haven't slept with him. And believe me, I could have. You throw yourself at him as soon as you see him and expect him to want you? That doesn't make you classy, doll, it makes you a whore!"

We left and headed to my spot. "I'm so proud of you Tara. Way to put those bitches in check."

Dylan came up behind Tara and wrapped his hands around her, kissing her neck and shoulders. "Let's get out of here, doll. I want you all to myself." She had a huge smile on her face. The Barbie twins had seen it and stormed off.

As the show ended, Gavin told me to go grab a drink while he took what was left to the truck. I sat at the bar just thinking about how awesome the night had been. I had completed my first expo and done very well with it. Most of my copies had sold, and people took cards for KC's. Having Tara there to talk to people about the shop was smart. She raked in a few new clients. Three different modeling agents approached her, and she was asked to do a spread in *Lady*

Tattoo Magazine. I told her if she made it big because of my pictures, I wanted a black and purple Harley Davison. Too bad the Barbie twins didn't see her talking to the agents; that would have been priceless.

It was just after 11 o'clock, and even though I was beyond tired, Winston and Tyler were meeting us at my house at midnight. I knew there were times when I should have said no when it came to hanging out, but I hadn't figured out how to do that yet.

A tall, muscular, Italian man came and sat next to me. His big smile matched his Jersey Shore cockiness. He was handsome and dressed in a navy blue, three-piece, designer suit. "Can I buy you a drink? You look like a Malibu kind of girl, nice and sweet."

"Actually, I'm a Corona girl, and my fiancé will buy it for me. Don't act like you didn't see the ring; I saw you look at it."

"Oh, I saw it. The question is why would he let such a beautiful creature out of his sight? It leaves room for men like me to move in."

"Really. What kind of man is that?"

"Rich, mysterious, devastatingly handsome, and great in bed. Should I keep describing myself, or would you like to try?"

"Well, I won't lie, you are handsome, but you forgot egotistical and rude."

"Ouch, that hurts. Can you at least tell me your name?"

"I suppose that won't hurt." I looked at the bartender with a smile. "My name is the future Mrs. Gavin Price. Go find another target Mr. Ego."

The bartender slipped me a corona and laughed. "I've seen

girls shoo guys like him away, but that was classic. He really thought he was getting somewhere. He must be dumb as a post to think a woman with a rock like that would look twice at him. This is an art gallery not a night club." Her gaze went to my side. "You must be Mr. Gavin Price."

"I am."

"Well then,"—she raised her eyebrows at me and smiled—"he didn't have a chance. You've got yourself the sexiest guy in the room and his ring. Congrats to you both!"

Gavin's attitude and expression were a mix of anger and satisfaction all wrapped up in one. "Whose ass do I have to kick?"

"Down boy! There will be no ass kicking of any kind, but if you'd like to fondle me in front of that egotistical prick, by all means, mark your territory. We both know you want to." I moved to the barstool directly in view of Mr. Ego. "Sit down, lover boy. Let's show everyone who I belong to."

"Mmm… I like the sound of that, my little minx. What do you have in mind?"

"I want you to look at him while you slip your fingers inside me, then suck them clean."

"There's my naughty girl. I'll gladly show him who owns your sweet ass, just know I'm fucking you senseless as soon as we get home. I don't care who's at the house, I'm gonna tear that pussy up."

Mr. Ego's eyes met mine as Gavin pulled me into his chest. So many times he'd said I was his, that my body was his, and it wasn't t until this moment that I truly understood the strength of those words. The heat from his body radiated through his shirt, burning my back. What I imagined would be a simple push inside me to prove a point turned into me struggling to suppress my moans and whimpers as he finger fucked me right there under the bar. The look on his face was so dominant that Mr. Ego got up and left. He slid his long fingers out of me and slowly sucked my juices off. Chills ran down my spine. The thrill of it took my breath away.

"Take me home and fuck me, please Gavin."

My lust-filled eyes made him go to his dark place. Sliding a fifty to the bartender, he pulled me outside to the truck, pinning me against it. With his strong hands wrapped around my throat, he growled, "You taste so fuckin' good. Did you like that? Did you like being watched?"

"Yes. I loved it. "

"I knew you did. You were soaking wet. Get your sexy ass in my truck before I split you in two right here in this parking lot." He helped me into it and hopped in. "Buckle up!"

CHAPTER 21

Gavin

Adrenaline rushed through my veins, and my cock throbbed. Showing that asshole that she was mine made me feel like a damn king. Telling her was one thing, but showing another man was a whole new ballgame. I've had sex in public before, but it was just fucking for the thrill of being watched. Tonight was different; tonight was a mindfuck. "Claire, I'm not gonna lie to you, that was such a turn-on. Watching the look of defeat on his face, knowing that he wanted you and I had you, I felt like a damn alpha male." We pulled into the driveway. "I need to fuck you right now. I'll stop whenever you want, but I need to get rough tonight."

She jumped out of the truck and ran to toward the house, ripping her clothes off along the way. Stopping in front of the door, she turned to me, and falling to her knees, she gazed up at me. "Let's start here."

"Oh, my naughty little girl, what am I going to do with you?"

"Anything you want!"

"Touch yourself, make yourself cum for me. You'll be nice and ready when I decide to stuff you full of my big, fat cock."

The look on her face as she pleasured herself for me was beautiful. Raw lust and need filled her eyes. Oh, the things this woman did to me. Her back arched and her hips bucked as she rode her fingers. The delicious noises her body made were more than I could handle.

"Enough! It's time to ride my cock."

Pushing the door open, I pulled her naked body to the couch, undoing my pants along the way. She climbed on my lap and slowly lowered herself onto my dick. The way her warm, tight pussy felt squeezing and sliding up and down the full length of my thick shaft was enough to make me blow my load, but I wouldn't let that happen yet. I shoved two fingers in her mouth and didn't even have to tell her to suck them. She licked and sucked, deep throating them. Once they were soaked in her spit I reached down and spread her ass cheeks open. Her face lit up, and she screamed my name when my fingers entered her tight little asshole, first one, then adding another.

"Fuck yeah, Gavin, fill both holes, baby. I want to be your dirty whore."

Pushing her off me, I bent her over my knee, pulling her hair with one hand and spanking her with the other. "Did I give you permission to talk?" My hand cracked down so hard on her ass that my palm stung. "When we fuck like this you only speak when spoken to." It was then that I realized Ty and Winston were cuddled up on the love seat.

Winston laughed a little. "Looks like somebody's been a bad girl. Should we leave?"

Tyler smiled at him. "Don't worry, hon; they're closet freaks. I'm sure us being here will make him fuck her harder."

He looked at me. "Do you want us to stay, man?"

I nodded and brought my hand to her ass a final time before dropping her on all fours. Pounding into her while one hand was tight around her throat, the other wrapped tight in her hair, I could hear her screams echoing through the house. My cock was twitching, my balls full to the brim. "Who's tight little pussy is this? Who owns you, you sexy little bitch?"

"It's all yours. You own me!"

I saw Tyler's head bobbing up and down, sucking Winston like her life depended on it. His face told me he was ready, and he nodded toward Claire. It was like we were in each other's twisted minds. I nodded at him, letting him know he'd get what he wanted; he'd get what I had. Gripping her hips as I pushed into her, I shot a huge load deep into her pussy before whispering in her ear.

"He has a present for Tyler, and I want to see you girls share nicely."

Twirling my hair around in her fingers, my beauty sank against me as we cuddled in our bed. Back from our lust-driven state of mind, I wondered what was going through her head. I didn't even ask her permission before throwing her at another man. I asked her to do something I knew she'd never want to do on her own. I'd gone to my dark place, the unemotional part of me that ran purely on my own sick pleasure. I felt a tear run down my chest, then another, and another. Guilt ran through me, crushing me. What was I thinking? I wasn't, that's the problem.

"Please forgive me. I'll never ask you to do that again. I swear; I'll never even put us in that situation again. Just you and me baby, nobody else. I'm begging you, don't leave me, Claire." I felt more tears before she turned her back to me and curled into a ball. "Do you want me to leave?"

"No, I could have said no. I didn't stop it because I thought I'd like it. It was so much fun before. With you and Tyler, it was meant to be for fun, but there was real love and passion in it for me.

This time I just felt like a trashy whore. I feel dirty and I hate myself for it." Her tears fell like rain. "The sex was amazing, everything up to what happened with them was exactly what I wanted. I wanted them to watch us, not join us. I can't believe I had another man's cum in my mouth."

"It's my fault, sweetheart, I took it too far. Don't ever think of yourself that way. You are sweet and pure. I'm ruining you more and more each day, and I'm sorry."

I got up and put my clothes on, I needed to leave. She didn't want me there anyway. Looking back at her, I left without even saying goodbye. I had to figure out how to fix this, or if I even wanted to. She deserved better than me, better than what I am. I thought I could change, but the more she enjoyed what I showed her, the further I ended up taking her. I'd done exactly what I didn't want to do; I'd taken it too far.

I ended up at the beach, where we'd gone the night we became us. The sand was cold despite the warm weather, but lying in it made me feel close to her. Looking up at the moon, I thought about what she'd said about it, how it was the one thing we could look at together even when we weren't together. I wondered if she was looking at it, too. Was she thinking about me, about us? We had to get past this; she was my other half. I finally have her; I'm not about to let her go.

I turned around to go plead my case, to beg for forgiveness, and there she was. My love was standing in front of me. Our lips met in a reassuring, passionate kiss.

"I swear I didn't follow you. I guess we really are one person."

"Baby, I—"

"Don't you ever say you ruin me; you fixed me. You brought me back to life in every way. I love you and the things *we* do. You make me feel free. From now on, it's just me and you, nobody else." She stood on her toes and kissed my forehead. "And don't you ever walk out on me again."

"Marry me tomorrow, right here under the moon. I'm not waiting any longer. Just you, me, my parents, and Miles. We can still have the party on Saturday, a bonfire in the backyard with a handful of people. We'll bust out the grill and have what we call fun. What do you say?"

"Yes! Oh, my God *yes*!"

CHAPTER 22

Claire

Looking in the mirror, I wondered what my mother would have thought. She had been so happy helping me get ready to walk down the aisle with Cole. She adored him. When cancer took her from me, Cole and I were still in love, and he had never even raised his voice to me. She never saw him become the monster my father was. My father beat my mother senseless until she left him. I'm just glad she met Audrey before she passed.

A knock on the door snapped me back to reality. "May I come in?"

"Of course, Mrs. Price. Are you ready for me to steal your boys?"

"I'm ready to get the daughter I always wanted. I prayed for the day my son would find a good woman. I know he was unhappy with the life he was leading. He never told me about anything, but a mother knows when her son is hurting. Once he met you, it all changed; the closer you got to him, the happier he was." Tears ran down my cheeks. "Thank you for being a mother to my grandson. He loves you so much. I don't want to make you cry away your makeup, so let's go. Oh, and stop calling me Mrs. Price, I'm your mother now."

"Okay, Mom!"

While we drove to the beach, I thought about how mad Tyler

and Tara were going to be, but they'd get over it. The beautiful moon was full and bright, so perfect for the night. My dress blew in the wind as my soon-to-be mother in-law escorted me to the shoreline. I saw them all, Tyler and Tara on my side, and Winston and Dylan next to Gavin. I tried so hard not to cry.

"Let's go make you my real mommy!" Miles popped down from the lifeguard chair he'd been sitting on with Gavin's father.

"You look so handsome, love bug!"

Standing in front of the people who mean the most to us and the two new additions to our circle, we said our vows, made our promises, and shared a kiss of true love. It was the most amazing and romantic moment of my life.

"Wake up, Mr. Price; you're going to be late for work. I'll get the monster up and moving."

"Excuse me, Mrs. Price, but we are staying in bed all day so I can ravage you over and over. You'll be walking crooked by the time I get done with you!"

"As much as I'd love that, we have to get up and get Miles to school. Let's let Miles stay at the shop with Tara after school and come home and take away his title of only child." Nibbling Gavin's chin, I climbed on top of him. "How about a quick head start right now?" I felt him get hard instantly. "I see someone's rising to the occasion."

"Mommy, Daddy, time to wake up! I need to go tell all my friends I have a real mommy now."

"Okay, buddy, you win. I'll be down in a second to get your breakfast."

"I just got cockblocked by my own kid; this sucks." He lifted the blanket to show me his erection.

Pulling the covers over my head, I giggled. "Well, lucky for you, I suck, too."

I went back to the shop to put in a solid days work. I wanted to try and see if I could set up some sort of event for MILES OF COMICS, an official grand opening celebration. Tara was working on a tattoo of an Army tank in front of an American flag on the back of an extremely hot soldier. I'm not usually attracted to the clean-cut type, but this guy was an exception. His short, thick, black hair and flawless, olive-colored skin were a perfect contrast to his bright blue eyes. His chiseled chest muscular arms were impossible not to stare at. He was eye candy at its finest and practically throwing himself at Tara. He had just gotten back from Iraq and was telling her about it. Tara's father was a Navy SEAL, so they were exchanging jokes back and forth about which was better. He was clearly flirting with her, but she's so insecure she didn't even pick up on it. I thought having Dylan show so much interest in her would give her a little more self-confidence, but it didn't.

Dylan and Tara are a complicated pair. He seems to worship the ground she walks on, but she doesn't see it. He doesn't even care that she's not interested in sex. He could get it from so many girls with the snap of a finger, but he only wants her. Maybe she really isn't interested and is keeping her distance so he doesn't get the wrong idea. Who knows?

"So, is there a lucky man who gets to come home to you?"

"Not exactly." Her face turned bright red as she glanced over at me.

"Well, that's good."

"Why is that good, Mr. Roberts?"

"Well, first of all, call me Adam. Second, if there were someone really special, then you would have a ring on your finger. If there's just a boyfriend, then there's room for me to sneak in and steal you, in the most respectful way, of course."

"How is that in any way respectful?" She was laughing at how he'd raised one eyebrow at her.

"A woman's heart can be stolen from another man without being disrespectful to him. Charm and honesty go a long way, darlin'. The heart wants what the heart wants. I'd never touch a woman until she ended the relationship. That, beautiful, is where the respect comes into play."

"Well, there's no official relationship to end, but I've been seeing someone for the last two weeks. Honestly, I'm not sure what we are or where either one of us wants to be."

"Is that your way of telling me you'll let me take you on a date?"

"Let's just say I'll think about it. Your number is on the form you signed. Maybe I'll give you a call."

She put the tattoo gun down and cleaned him up. "All done. What do you think?"

"It's perfect, just like you."

"Thanks, it was nice meeting you, Adam."

"I hope I hear from you soon, Tara."

I saw her shake her head at herself in the mirror before

handling her equipment. I loved seeing her smile, but all I could think of was Dylan. She wasn't doing anything wrong, but I knew he'd be upset if she called this guy.

"Tara, what's up with Captain America?"

"Not a damn thing. I'm not calling him, but playing Little Miss Sunshine got me a big fat tip! I'm not doing anything to make Dylan run away. I might be confused about us, but I like him a lot."

"Why are you so confused? I mean he's clearly into you. Why do you keep him at arm's length?

"I don't know. I guess I'm afraid that I'll fall for him and then he'll meet some beautiful actress, and it's goodbye Tara."

The door opened and in walked Sammie; I'd totally forgotten about her coming. Tara had her sit at the table and prepped her for her tattoo. I waved and headed toward the comic shop; I had no desire to be around her. Poor Tara had no choice but to be nice and talk to her.

"Okay, let's do this. When did you get the original one done?"

"About nine years ago. It was a spur of the moment thing. I like the idea of my son's name thrown into it."

"Me too. It's funny that he has the same name as Claire's son. It's not a very common name for little boys nowadays."

"I didn't think she had kids, just a step-son."

She was starting to piss me off so I stepped in on the conversation. "Well, my husband has a five-year-old son whose mother bailed on him as a newborn. Genetics don't matter to us; he's my son."

"What are you going to do if his real mother comes back?"

I couldn't believe she had the nerve to say that. "Not that it's any of your business, but she signed over all parental rights to Gavin when Miles was two months old. Even if she tried to, she couldn't get him back. Any woman who'd walk away from their child like she did doesn't deserve breath. She's a selfish cunt if you ask me. I'm his real mother now."

The door opened and Miles bounced into my arms. "Mommy, I missed you!"

Gavin's face dropped when he walked in. "Samara, what the *fuck* are you doing here?"

I looked at her then at Gavin. "Mara, your ex-wife?"

Tara stood up and jumped back. "You've gotta be shittin' me! She's your ex?"

Sammie laughed. "I couldn't very well introduce myself as Mara, so I went with Sammie. Now what were you saying about me being a selfish cunt?"

"You heard me. It's been you following me around, hasn't it, you crazy fuckin' bitch?" I put Miles down and kissed him. "Go next door and stay with Aunt Tyler, buddy. Don't you come back until I call you."

Gavin started yelling; I'd never heard him sound so angry. "Get the fuck out of here. Why would you do this to him, you piece of shit?"

"Because he's mine. I'm his mother."

"You walked out on him. You threw him away. You don't mean shit to him. He has a mother."

She grabbed her purse as if she was going to leave but pulled out small handgun. I saw Tara grab her phone before running to the back. She pointed the gun at Gavin but spoke to me. "I warned you. I told you he was mine." She began to laugh like a crazy person. "Did you think I meant Gavin? You did, didn't you? I left him, sweetie. He's all yours. He's a pussy who forgot how to fuck; I need a man who runs shit in bed. You can't have my son, though."

Gavin stepped toward her, "Samara, just put down the gun and leave. Don't be stupid. Legally, you have no claim to him."

She cocked the hammer. "Well, the thing about genetics is that if I kill you, he's mine. It's too late for this to go any other way, Gavin. Tell your wife to back off."

His body language hid the fear I saw in his eyes. "What are you gonna do? Kill us all and run away with him? He doesn't have a damn clue who you are. You're fucking insane."

I ran at her and grabbed the gun, pushing it up. She fired two rounds before I got it from her. I had pinned her to the ground and slid the gun away, and I kept hitting her over and over. It was as if I'd left my body and was watching myself. I kept saying, "He's my son." I saw Tara sitting in the corner with the phone to her ear. Sammie was still, so I ran to Gavin. He was hurt bad, she'd shot him twice. I held him close. "It's okay, baby. The ambulance is coming."

Tara screamed "Claire, look out!"

The gun was pressed to the back of my head. I stood and turned to her, with the gun in my face. I smiled.

"I won't kill you if you walk away. Step aside now. Only he needs to die."

I don't know what I was thinking, or if I even was, but I laughed. "Have you ever played chess, bitch? The queen always protects her king! I'm not going anywhere."

She began to lower the gun. "I shot him twice already. He's going to bleed out soon."

She had let her guard down, because she didn't even notice Cole and Morgan come in with guns drawn. Morgan shouted at her. "Put the gun down, Mara; place it on the floor and put your hands in the air."

Cole approached Mara with his gun pointed at her. I looked at Gavin as she lowered the gun to the ground. Cole cuffed her and started reading her rights to her. Backup pulled in as Morgan secured the scene and ran to Gavin. He applied pressure on the wounds, trying to comfort him as the ambulance pulled in. "You're gonna be all right, man. Your punk ass can't die on me. "

Cole handed Mara off to another officer and hugged me tight. "I promised you I'd keep you safe. He'll be okay, let's follow them, and Tyler can bring your son to the hospital once things have calmed down."

I grabbed Gavin's hand before they put him in the ambulance. "Why are you smiling? You have two bullets in you."

"I didn't know you played chess."

"I don't, but it sounded pretty badass, didn't it?" I giggled a bit. "Let's get you all patched up, Mr. Price." I kissed his forehead.

"Sweeter than a thousand, Mrs. Price."

THE END

COMING SOON…

Believe In Me

Tara & Dylan's story

Made in the USA
Columbia, SC
19 January 2024